W9-AES-267

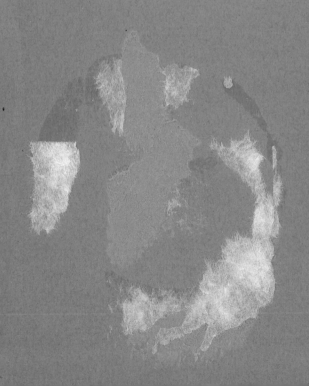

*Tenants of the House*

HEATHER ROSS MILLER

*Tenants of the House*

HARCOURT, BRACE & WORLD, INC. · NEW YORK

The lines from "Gerontion" by T. S. Eliot on page vii are from *Collected Poems 1909-1962* by T. S. Eliot, copyright, 1936, by Harcourt, Brace & World, Inc.; copyright © 1963, 1964 by T. S. Eliot.

*for* GENEVA *and* FRED ROSS

*Gull against the wind, in the windy straits*
*Of Belle Isle, or running on the Horn.*
*White feathers in the snow, the Gulf claims,*
*And an old man driven by the Trades*
*To a sleepy corner.*

*Tenants of the house,*
*Thoughts of a dry brain in a dry season.*

T. S. ELIOT, "GERONTION"

# One

F OLKS IN JOHNSBORO said old Preacher Murdoch was not a happy spirit and that his ghost walked the mountain, looking out for something. They had asked him once, somebody remembered it at his death, "Preacher, do you believe in ghosts?"

He had stopped walking and stood with one hand on his stick (those strange walking sticks that he found in the woods, searching patiently until he found a sapling wound round and round in vines, twisted in a pattern of hard spirals). The other hand was on his hip and he leaned forward slightly.

"Well," he said, his Scotch accent rolling out upon them in a heavy river. He frowned in the sun. "Well, brothers, the Scriptures speak of witchcraft and wandering spirits." And then he walked away, leaving them blinking and feeling silly in the sun. They hadn't really expected an answer of him. They considered Preacher Murdoch something of an oddity, a bit touched, living up there on the mountain all alone and pronouncing his words so funny. He was an outsider. Even though this town of Johnsboro had begun in the wane of the nineteenth century, a few years after the Confederate war, when John Murdoch, Presbyterian minister by trade and poor Scot by birth, crossed the Yadkin on a cotton barge and came ashore in the shadow of a pine-dark Nantahala mountain. Being Presbyterian and leader of his flock, and having descended from a long line of Scottish shepherds who tended their sheep on the banks of the Clyde, John Murdoch felt called to build a house of refuge by this wide and rolling river Yadkin. So, astride a lean sorrel which he had bought before his crossing, picking his way through the flinty hills of Nantahala and riding through the red soil of the Yadkin valleys, John Murdoch gathered enough poor farmers and settlers to help raise the beams of his holy place, which he called Murdoch's Mission, a name shortened in years simply to Mission.

When he was young, his father had taken him to Glasgow, that royal city by the sea, the queen of the Clyde. And the stout old Scot had said, "Beware of cities and women. The Lord has said."

The life of the shepherd was the best life. It was hard, but it was the best. The smell of the sheep, of mutton and of wool, the smell of the pasture grass in the sun: these were good to the boy John. And as he lay at night under a sky thick with stars, the herd like a ghostly murmuring cloud, and he listened to the Clyde rushing down to the sea, he thought of how he should become a shepherd of men. He never forgot the sound of the Clyde and the night stars and the sheep. And when he became a man he took the black frock of the minister and made his way to the American shores.

It was his plan to establish here in the Carolina wilderness, where so many of his Scots had come before him, a new Canaan with himself at the head of the fold, to gather, to lead, and to shield. It would be he, John, beloved of our Lord, who would guide these humble folk into a state of grace. Under his gentle but firm hand, they would receive the water of baptism, they would drink the pure unfermented juice of the grape in commemoration of Christ-blood. He would wed them, christen their babes, and repeat over them the chants of burial. All in the bosom of this holy place.

> *. . . I shall call my walls* SALVATION!

But it didn't turn out that way. The vision that burned under the carbide lamps of the Carolina farmers as John Murdoch stood in their kitchens and talked of his church, his Mission, burned in the lamp of Destiny with a different blaze struck by another match.

The vision conceived under the Scottish night sky was not safe from cities and women. No matter what the Lord had said. It was doomed from the moment John Murdoch set foot on Palmer County soil. In the first place, he was an idealist in the midst of hardened realists. They would be glad to help him build a church and they would faithfully attend it in the face of storms and fever. They had been trained to fear God from the cradle. But they had been in the wilderness long enough to know that making a living took all a man. What little bit there might be left over was all they could spare to God. They came and sat on wooden benches and listened to John Murdoch saying,

> *Come unto me, all ye that labour and are heavy laden, and I will give you rest.*

And their muscles ached from the day before and would ache again on the morrow.

Canaan was not safe from spies. The fold was broken. The vision spread itself and opened like a fan. And the river brought them all: new farmers, coopers, millers, smiths, even new preachers rivaling John Murdoch for the flocks of God. The people smelled of sweat and mules and new lumber. And there were women. Women with colors of red and gold, beautiful and delicate as poison lilies, with such enduring and powerful loveliness, blossoming where least expected. They stood and held their babies on hip or waited in doorways. John Murdoch felt his evangelism begin to wither and he watched the petals drop off one by one.

He had crossed the Clyde, the Yadkin. But the land beyond the Jordan was forbidden him. He stood on the bluffs of the wilderness river and watched the brown-red water wind through Nantahala and he became obsessed by the thought that it was through water all evil must have originally come to man. Water. The eternal female symbol. The fount of all knowledge. The water and the woman and the serpent. And Eden was no more.

John Murdoch wanted only one thing after he saw Canaan overrun, and that was to have his Mission, at least, undisturbed. Instead, these strangers took both his Mission and his name. To the thriving village, they gave his Christian name: Johnsboro. And to the dark mountain that shadowed the village, they gave his clan name: Murdoch. He continued, though, to cling to his last bare dream and prayed that he might preach out the rest of his days in Mission. But after all his years of work and hope and complete dismay, the Carolina synod sent a young man barely out of Fayetteville Seminary to take his place. *His place!* John Murdoch could not bear the sight of that young man standing in his pulpit each Sunday, his face that still had a baby roundness to the cheek and chin, the skin so red from a razor that he seemed a grotesque branch of the gladiola bouquet upon the altar table.

So he left and went to live on his mountain, the one called Murdoch's, in a bare wooden house that didn't have room for visions. He lived there with no wife to share his old age and no children to comfort him. Mission had been his spouse, his seed. And Mission was no more. He died, unattended, on a beautiful summer afternoon, while birds chattered in the forest and the giant magnolia that grew in his dooryard opened forth its thick fragrance on the shimmering sunlight. He had been drawing water at his well and as he pulled the bucket brimming to the well curb, the water sloshed over, staining the stone dark blue. He set the bucket to one side and took the dipper from its nail. There was a tiny spot of rust on the bowl of the dipper and as he lifted it to his lips, John Murdoch suddenly began to laugh. He laughed and laughed and the sound of his laughter filled the hot afternoon and echoed over the dark green mountain.

"Oh, God!" he said weakly, exhausted with laughing, and bent to sit on the ground by the well. His head tipped back against the slate, not so dark blue any more, slowly drying with the sun. Through half-closed eyes, as through a dim fringe, a veil of dust, he saw her coming, with her pitcher on her shoulder. Dark-eyed, with bracelets of gold upon her arms, she paused before him. The pitcher was red, as red as rust in the sunlight, and the dark eyes of the damsel glowed. Oh, whore of Babylon, mother of God, let down thy pitcher, I pray thee, that I may drink. And she said, in a tiny voice that hushed the birds and stupefied the fragrant air, she said, Drink, my lord: and she hasted, and let down her pitcher upon her hand, and gave him drink.

Oh, Rebekah, thou art my sister, be thou my mother, my wife, and let my seed possess the gate of those which hate me.

His hand fell limp upon the grass and the spotted dipper dangled from his fingers.

Despite the unhappy spirit of John Murdoch, his village grew and changed easily, almost too easily. Perhaps the real changes, the ones that could be seen in buildings and pavements as well as in strange faces and new names, came with the aluminum people. They were a French company, L'Aluminium Français. And they had ambitious plans to dam the water of the Yadkin and raise a smelter on its banks. They drew out the usual zones for Business and for Residence, laid foundations for the smelter, and began construction on a mud dike before they were called home to fight French wars against a Kaiser.

After the war, the French company was left bankrupt and so another aluminum company, this one from Illinois, purchased the town and smelter sites, the water rights, the mud dike, everything from L'Aluminium Français, and then proceeded to construct the dwellings, lay out the streets, raise the smelter, dam the Yadkin, and even plant the shrubbery exactly as the French had designed.

The people of Johnsboro looked on and accepted the changes just as their forefathers had accepted the sun and the hail, Jesus Christ, taxes, and river typhoid. After all, they told one another, this new aluminum business and that dam meant new jobs and more money, running water in the kitchens, electric lights, and maybe even telephones for everybody. But when the newcomers, the new visionaries, suggested that the name of the town be changed to honor some company official long-buried back in Illinois, the native folk stubbornly objected. That much they did for John Murdoch, whether they realized it or not. They could suffer Yankees in their bosoms, even perhaps in their beds, but they could never have this hard-won Southern soil called by a Yankee name.

So Johnsboro kept its name and its legend. But in all other aspects it soon became a company town. The French apartments went up, all exactly alike in color, shape, and view. As they faced one another up and down the coves of Nantahala, they bore not the slightest mark of individuality, except for their numbers, which were painted in neat black over the lintel of every door: No. 86 (on the left side of the street), No. 87 (on the right side of the street), No. 88 (again on the left), and so on throughout the entire town. Like a beehive, it rose, chamber upon chamber, and sealed itself.

Strangers to Johnsboro got lost and were confused by the

identical apartments spread out around the narrow streets that were crisscrossed at corners by cement drainage ditches or graveled back alleys. It was as elaborate as an Elizabethan garden and more maddening than a labyrinth. All this was greatly changed in the passing years and the stern honeycomb was softened by the planting of rosebushes and obelia, the erecting of white pickets or trellised arbors, the steady blossoming of children around the doorways and in the small green yards. Johnsboro became a pretty little village.

Even the identical architecture didn't matter so much anymore. The people came to like it and to be somewhat proud. It gave them something that they could say, to outsiders, was certainly different from the other little towns in Palmer County, or perhaps in the whole state of North Carolina.

The aluminum smelter sat on the edge of Johnsboro, big and impressive with giant smokestacks and long, flat rectangular potrooms, and an iron-fenced yard wherein lay the ingots, gleaming with a dull-white luster, waiting to be transported on the railway to Pittsburgh or Birmingham. The sign on the fence read PIEDMONT ALUMINUM, Smelting Division of THE ALUMINUM COMPANY OF ILLINOIS. Perched high on a bluff overlooking the lake were a tiny laboratory and the various company offices. And the lake itself was a large, irregularly shaped portion of muddy water that had flowed up with the damming of the Yadkin. It was called, misappropriately, Lake John. There were in the end three dams instead of one, and all three took their names from familiar landmarks and water signs: The Narrows, The Falls, and The High Rock. These massive barriers that were wedged into the channels of the strong red river and flanked against the hills of Nantahala, these fortresses commanded the watercourses to move steel and strike current, increase pressure and ignite the glowing white friction that sped electricity into the potlines of the smelter. And then aluminum, the bluish-white metal found only in locked combination in nature, was separated from its salts and poured off into ingots, light and malleable, resistant to oxidation and convenient to melt and reshape.

The Yadkin water that gave birth to John Murdoch's mission also gave birth to Piedmont Aluminum. After a gestation long and complicated, Johnsboro opened its eyes to the 1940's from under a cradle shawl embroidered in fox fire, God, and electricity. Its childhood was sheltered. And the gold-winged guardian angels that hover unseen in the darkness behind a child's bed somehow managed to sprinkle a few bright feathers over Johnsboro.

The people who lived in the beehive answered the whistles of Piedmont Aluminum and went to work on time, punched the electrolytic pots, cut the carbon, watched the dials and gauges that opened and closed the turbines, operated pulleys and railways and poured off the molten aluminum. They measured and compared the purity of their metal in the tiny laboratory over Lake John. They took salt tablets to reimburse their bodies for the sweat the potrooms took away. They recorded invoices and tabulated inventories. They typed and stamped and telegraphed. They kept charts on the fluctuation of the Yadkin, the red overflow of the three dams. They sat in the guardhouse and patrolled the night streets of Johnsboro. All this they did, and then clocked out and went home. It was a way of life.

There is something about a dollhouse that evokes in its beholder the feelings of omnipotence, of being God. He gazes and gazes upon the view, at each of the rooms, the little partitions, the peculiar slanting roof, and he knows it is too perfect. The people wouldn't live in it that way with all the furniture arranged so neatly, no toys scattered on the floor, no grease spattering in the kitchen, and no warm print of love upon the bed. The painted ivy climbs across the tin verandah and a yellow fire burns silently within the cold hearth. Johnsboro looked very much like a doll town made of dollhouses. But its people were very much imperfect, as real people should surely be. And so was the God who beheld them.

# Two

Somewhere around six the newspapers thumped against the doorsteps of the apartments on Lee Street. The paper boy, Adam Rich, glided through the early mist, pedaling his red bicycle languidly. Adam was half-asleep, humped over the handlebars. Then, as he approached another doorstep, he straightened, reached behind to pull a rolled-up paper from the canvas swung across his back wheel, and "thwump," with all the accuracy of a bowman, Adam flung the paper toward No. 42, a flank of brick steps lined in boxwood, or toward No. 44, a concrete ledge with daffodils on either side.

It was proper that his name should be Adam, the first man, awake in these misty hours, alone and moving through the quiet street. He held dominion over the shadowy trees and the apartments still locked in slumber. As the windowpanes began to redden in the sun that was rising behind Murdoch's Mountain, Adam turned the corner and was gone.

In his wake the redness spread swiftly through the thick forest and over the grey honey-celled cement of Johnsboro and into the first rooms on Lee Street. The people were awakening.

In No. 42, a middle-of-the-row apartment, upstairs in a bedroom with three large windows and a dormer alcove, Michael Glenn turned toward the sleeping figure of his wife, Linda Earl, and put out his hand. The moment before his fingers brushed the curve of her shoulder, he took them back. Linda Earl hated to be bothered in the morning, before she had to. And already he had heard Darryl pittypatting down the hall outside their door. After a little while, the child started downstairs, one step and one stocky foot at a time, plop-plop, literally dragging himself behind him. Michael lay on his side, gazing out at the brightening sky and listening to his son go down the stairs. Halfway down, Darryl stopped and sat. "Twinkle, twinkle, little star," he sang heartily, "how I wonder what you are!"

Linda Earl flopped around, pulling the sheets over her head and muttering, "Oh, for goodness sake." Her voice was fuzzy with sleep and her dark lashes still tight against waking. Her shoulder touched Michael's back and as she lay there feeling warm and cozy against him, she began to doze again.

"Linda," he wanted to say tenderly. "Linda, did you know that once, oh, it was a long time ago, and, oh, it was so damned silly. But once I wanted to be like Daniel Boone. Did you know that?" Michael Glenn was asleep again, too. "Linda, I even checked a book out of the library once. It was *The Pathfinder* and I never thought I could get through all of that big book. But I did. And from then on I wanted to be a pathfinder and discover new places."

The three large windows blazed crimson with sunrise and the bedclothes turned silken. The whole room wavered and swam in rich deep dreamings, as rich and thick as old honey.

"Michael, it is time for my piano lesson. Granny says every lady of quality must learn how to play the piano so as to be able to play in church someday. Here is Miss Campbell. We are alone in the parlor, I on the piano stool, the one with claws holding a big glass marble, and she on a straight-backed chair from the dining room. Outside my brothers are getting up the hay. I can see them through the window. Billy stands on the wagon and Hoyle throws up a bale. Then the wagon moves on as Billy whistles to the mule. 'Darling, this is a wonderful garden. And that is the way we must think of the piano. As a wonderful garden that our fingers can unlock!' "

"I dreamed of climbing new mountains, ones with snow on the top and caves thick with ice, and maybe even old bones. I would pass into new valleys where no man had ever gone before me. I wanted to sit in the woods at night and look at the stars (it would be a pitch-black night and they would be burning-bright stars) and know that I was the first, the onliest man who had sat in those woods and looked up at those stars."

"And every Wednesday she came to teach me the piano. One time it was very hot and we had to raise the windows and the wind kept blowing all the music off the piano. So I sat on it and held the piece we were playing down with two hymnals. And when my lesson was over and I stood up, the music stuck to the backs of my legs. I had on a short pinafore dress and it stuck all the way up to where my panties were."

The redness and the honey-soft slumber suddenly shifted and broke. A dart of sunlight pierced Michael's eye and he turned to escape it. But instead of the tender darkness he turned for, he felt instantly the irritability of his wife tremble through their bed and when he took down the sheet from her face, he saw only the pout of her lips and the reluctance in her eyes as she waked to his touch.

"Go get him, Michael," she said, raising up on one elbow and yawning in the sunlight. "He's going to wake up Carolyn and then I'll never be able to fix breakfast on time."

To fix breakfast and on time. That was the important thing, the only thing to Linda Earl this morning. In the wilderness a man need not eat his breakfast on time. And his breakfast, dammit, it could be as wild and as raw as his spirit.

Michael got out of bed and drew on his robe. The feel of it sent a slight shiver through his skin. As he opened the door, Carolyn began fussing in her crib across the hall.

Linda Earl drew in her breath and said grumpily, "Oh, this happens every morning sure as the world!"

He closed the door. At the end of the short hall was another window, this one small and square, each pane limned precisely in black. Michael went toward it and as he stood there the bright blueness of the sky, as blue as a steel blade freshly honed, cleaved Linda Earl from his mind. He felt the blood rise in his heart as a bird flew out from the eaves breaking the air with his wings.

"Hey, Daddy."

He looked over at Darryl, sitting in a little heap of yellow flannel on the stairs.

"Come on, bud."

Michael put the boy on his shoulder and jogged downstairs and out to get the paper that Adam had thrown on the step earlier. After breakfast, he sat at the table looking through the paper. He turned a page and read MORE TROOPS LEAVE BRAGG. A little farther on was a picture of three children standing with spades in their hands. The caption said LOCAL CHILDREN PLANT VICTORY GARDEN. And next to that was SCRAP METAL EFFORT GAINS SUPPORT THROUGHOUT N.C. He put it down wearily. Darryl was hammering with a mixing spoon on the leg of the table. Linda Earl stood with the baby on her hip, warming a bottle of milk in a pan on the stove. In the sunlight let in from the windows to the left of the table where Michael sat, she looked like a drawing in yellow water paint done on rice paper, partly washed away. She was scattered in white, a smudge of sepia for her long hair, and her body was patched together with intense and brilliant spots of India ink. The baby's head bobbed with tiny blotches of gold.

"Oh, for heaven's sake, Darryl! Hush that racket." She

turned and Michael was startled to see that her face was only a dark blob in the midst of so much light. The kitchen was a negative with the darks and the lights suddenly reversed. He blinked his eyes. Linda Earl was saying something.

". . . and if you could get me somebody to tend the children, then maybe I could work over there. Mrs. Kulp said . . ."

"What!" Michael stood up and stretched, feeling the segments of his spine tighten, then relax. "You thinking about working again? You know I don't like it, Linda, why do you keep on? I make enough for us. Even as good as your old man ever did."

He knew he had hurt her. He had meant to.

"Well." She picked up the baby's bottle and shook it. "I just wanted to help some." Her voice was weak, tearful, the thin rending of a rose petal.

Michael felt sorry now and went over and took the baby. He kissed the fuzzy golden head and held her up high, making her laugh. The round blue eyes twinkled, as blue as bits of wilderness sky seen through leaf spray.

"You can help me lots more by tending to these kids and being here when I come home than you can by working in some damned mill all day long."

Linda Earl shook out some milk on her wrist. The white drops quivered, then she rubbed them away defiantly. "Okay," she said and smiled up. "Okay." The points of the rose furled inward.

In the next apartment Christa Kulp had been awake for a long time. She'd seen Adam come with the papers and, after Adam, Mr. Greene the milkman. Mr. Greene drove a white truck shaped just like a white waxy box and painted on the side in meadow-green letters was GREENE'S DAIRY. When he stepped out of the waxy box, Mr. Greene was clothed all in white and his glasses sparkled in the sun like a just-washed milk bottle. He used to have a delivery boy that would run out with the milk while Mr. Greene waited in the truck keeping the motor on. But since the war had started, all the delivery boys had gone. Christa wondered if they had gone to the war. No one ever said.

She sat in the window looking out over Lee Street. If Mama knew it, she would have a fit. "Sitting in the window, street-wards, with nothing on but your 'jamas!" But Mama was in the next room getting dressed for work. Christa could hear her parents talking softly as they got ready for the day. It wasn't hard to hear through the thin apartment walls.

"I guess you'll find out for sure about Rebecca at work today. Old lady Byrd was sure upset last evening. Could hear her squawling all over the block."

"Well, I guess maybe she was. And she didn't care who knew it either." There was a short silence. There were the sounds of the bed being made and the pillows plumped. "But it was to be expected, though, Jim. The way they went on all the time. Rebecca being just as nice and kind and obliging as any human person could be. And that old woman always picking, picking, and bossing the living daylights out of the girl."

There was another pause and Christa could picture how her mother, Rose Kulp, had stopped talking and was looking off blankly and piously into the distance of all four corners of the room. She was now shaking her head and continuing. "And such a nice girl. Why, Jim, a prettier, nicer girl, God never put breath into."

"Well, the old lady is to be pitied more than scorned. But she's really got worse since Bill died. You remember how she . . ."

"Jim, we better hush now. The children might be listening. And I thought I heard Christa stirring awhile ago anyhow. Let's go down."

Christa got out of her window. She dressed for school and as she dressed she thought about Rebecca. Rebecca Byrd with long black hair floating about her white shoulders and her eyes as black and brilliant as jet. She was lovely and when she laughed, her mouth trembled startlingly scarlet against the whiteness of her face. Skin as white as snow, hair as black as ebony, lips as red as blood. She was that Princess Snowdrop in the old story.

Rebecca and her mother lived in the apartment opposite the Kulps'. Theirs was gloomy and grey, covered over in thick cudzu vines. Mrs. Wallace, who had lived next to the Byrds, complained once about the cudzu. And when old lady Byrd told her to shut up and to keep her hands off the cudzu, there had developed a great feud between them. Mrs. Wallace tacked a white cord up the side of the apartment wall and any cudzu that grew over the cord was whacked off and thrown over to Mrs. Byrd's side to wilt and turn brown in the sun. When the paint crew came to whiten the apartments of Lee Street, they tried to tear down the vines to get at the walls beneath. And, while Mrs. Wallace stood in her door laughing, poor Mrs. Byrd ran them away with her broom. And though the other apartments took on a fresh coat of white and got their windows, doors, and porches trimmed in green, the Byrd apartment remained stubbornly grey and dingy and the cudzu thrived.

Christa buttoned on a plaid dress and laced her brown oxfords. Then she rolled up her pajamas into a hard little knot and stuck them under the pillow the way she'd been taught. She took a brush and sat in the window again, brushing her long copper hair, and looking across at the apartment where Rebecca had slept and wakened all her life and for as long as Christa herself could remember. The cudzu was brilliantly green this morning and nodded innocently in the air. The feud had ended with Mrs. Wallace's death. But just a month before, while Christa and her little sisters were helping finish up the dishes one evening, Mrs. Byrd knocked on the door and when Jim answered, had said "I want to use your telephone." Not "May I use it," but "I want it." Anyhow, Jim Kulp had consented and when the old woman picked up the receiver, she turned to him and Rose and with a wave of her hand included the girls in the kitchen.

"Now, you all be a witness to this."

She asked the operator for Mrs. Wallace's number and when the woman answered, shouted at the top of her voice into the telephone, "GO TO HELL, YOU DAMN FOOL HUSSY!" And then, later, at Mrs. Wallace's funeral, Mrs. Byrd had appeared, alone and tight-lipped, dressed in a baggy blue suit with a rhinestone brooch on the lapel. The only comment she had to make on the deceased was "Pollie Wallace would be here today if she'd had as much sense as her neighbors." No one ever really ciphered the meaning of these words. Mrs. Wallace had died of acute pneumonia. So perhaps what Mrs. Byrd meant was that a growth of thick cudzu acted as an insulation against cold winds and tempests. But who really knew.

Anyhow, Rebecca was not like her mother. She was friendly to everybody and spoke in a soft voice. Even when her mother was raging the fiercest, Rebecca only turned gracefully and smiled and said, "Mother, you're talking loud and you're talking fast and you haven't *said* anything yet."

The smell of Rebecca was the smell of little violets that first spring up in April. Or she was the smell of the rain on sweet dark earth, dropping on leaves, shimmering in crystal splinters through the cudzu vine on the grey apartment house. And when the sun came out again, it shone through the raindrops and illuminated the cudzu in a fiery spider's web.

This then was Rebecca Byrd: the rain and the violets and the reappearing sunlight. Electricity crackled in Christa's brush and the ends of her hair curled slightly. She stopped brushing and leaned with her elbows on the sill, staring hard at the apartment across the street. What had Rebecca done to cause such a commotion, to make Mama whisper about her in the next room and then hush off for fear of being overheard? Christa hoped Rebecca had run away in the middle of the night, climbing down the cudzu vines, over the grey sides of the witch tower, her long black hair spread out in a cape behind her. Christa Kulp closed her eyes and saw Rebecca passing swiftly, leaving the scent of violets and the touch of damp black wings.

There was another who thought of Rebecca Byrd at this hour. His name was Eugene Boyette and he loved her. Gene Boyette was seventeen years old. Rebecca was nineteen. And he had loved her intensely since his first view of her two winters ago, standing naked in the kitchen, late a December evening. He had been returning from basketball practice. The darkness fell early and by the time Gene entered Lee Street a fluttering of snow blanketed his footsteps. As usual he cut through the back alleys behind Lee Street, where Hampton Street joined in and after Hampton, Stuart Street and home. Here in the alleys the ground was already soft with snow and the garbage cans wore a rim of whiteness. At the bend of the alley, Gene stopped to light a cigarette. The match flared for a moment in the cold and as it went out the dark seemed more intense. He leaned against someone's garage and looked around at the silent apartments behind him. Everything seemed asleep, lulled by the silence of the snow, deaf, immutable, colder than the stars. His eye scanned the length of them and he blinked for a moment. There in the corner of the last apartment was a small square of yellow light. As Gene looked at it longer, it appeared to grow brighter and also larger and after a while it seemed to move a bit to either side, like a signal lantern on a

long dark railroad. He blinked again and threw down the cigarette.

"Christ," he said, "these cigarettes are making me drunk."
He walked around the garage and looked back again at the
yellow light. He stepped onto the long sloping yard that led
up to the light. The snow broke under his shoes and the little
flakes stuck to his hair and along his lashes. Just below the
window was a huge obelia bush now shrouded by the snow.
Gene Boyette stood behind the obelia and gazed upwards.
There was Rebecca bathing from a pan of water on the stove.
The thin curtain that hung against the pane only enhanced her
nakedness.

> *Dark eyed,*
> *O woman of my dreams.*

Her hair was pinned up, but the steam had made little strands
of it fall down on her neck. They were sooty and damp and
clung to her gleaming skin.

> *. . . as a young sapling under the bark;*
> *. . . a river with lights.*

He stood and stood. He did not know how long he had
stood in the snow until he felt his feet beginning to go numb
with cold and his face tingle from the constant falling of the
flakes.

"Oh, God," he whispered in the darkness. "God, I am
drunk."

Rebecca moved inside in a yellow cubicle of warmth and
innocence. And when she had finished and switched off the
kitchen light, everything became cold and black again. There
was only the falling of the snow and the boy who stood outside the window.

> *Thy fingers a frosted stream.*

\*

The snow had melted and come again and melted again. And Gene Boyette loved Rebecca Byrd with all the silence and constant rhythmic reappearance of the snow. And she knew of it not at all. Gene she knew. But not his love. In fact, she had known Gene Boyette all her life. It was impossible to live in a town like Johnsboro and not know everybody. It was a plain sort of friendship with an outward crystal-sharp propriety. They saw each other at school and sometimes had walked home together after the Scout meetings on Wednesday evenings. They walked along, through the cellular streets, Gene in khaki and Rebecca in green gabardine, and they had talked of plain dull ordinary things. Then she was out of the Scouts, was graduated from high school and Gene never saw her again except on occasion in the grocery, at the post office, or on the vine-covered porch of her mother's apartment. And then there had come that weird night when the snow fell and he stood and watched through the window and his whole life had changed within him. He had begun to entangle himself with Rebecca Byrd, to perceive her, to reach out for her. And often as he sat in school looking out through the tall narrow windows at the apartments on Lee Street across from the schoolyard, he wondered what had really become of her.

And now he knew. He remembered that she had said something about wanting to go in training to be a nurse after her graduation. But the old lady, that disgusting old bag of a bitch, had put up such a howl that Rebecca gave way. But now Gene knew she had gone anyhow, despite the old lady's brawling. Alice, the Boyettes' serving girl, had brought him the news. She'd seen Rebecca downtown yesterday waiting for the bus from Fairview, a suitcase on either side of her. And the old lady had been there, too, hollering and scolding and puffing on those damned cigarettes. In fact, Alice said Mrs. Byrd had kept a fuss and a bother on until the bus pulled up and Rebecca got in and the driver shut the doors in Mrs. Byrd's face. Gene smiled to himself as he imagined how the last frowns and growls had probably been folded up like the bellows in an accordion and then squashed into wheezings under the tires of the bus.

The war was on in full fury and the government was training girls as nurses all over the country. Rebecca was free to go. It wouldn't cost Mrs. Byrd a dime. Gene wondered if he would have the guts to do such a thing as that. To just cut out like that and tell everybody to kiss your foot.

This morning he just tamely sat across the breakfast from his father, who was buttering a slice of toast and talking hurriedly.

"Elizabeth is feeling bad again this morning, son. She won't be down for breakfast. I expect you'd better drop by Doc Tracey's after school and get some more of those red pills. You don't need a prescription. I forget what the name is. Stami-Cine? Something like that. Anyhow, Doc'll know."

"Sure, Dad." Gene lifted his cup. The coffee steamed and he liked the feel of the vapor on his lip and the feel of the little cup handle in his fingers. It felt hard and smooth, as precise as a little white bone picked clean. The hot steamy feeling trickled down inside his body as he sat and looked across the table. Behind his father's head bloomed a long shelf of African violets. Elizabeth took great pride in raising African violets. She'd had that shelf built especially for them, up high, where they could be displayed to advantage. People passing in the street would look up and shake their heads and say, "Elizabeth Boyette has a knack for flowers. How *does* she do it?"

The violets were lovely this morning in the sunlight, lavender and blue and pink and milky-pearl, all shell-like with golden centers. The green leaves had pale whiskers and their undersides were softly veined. Elizabeth complained about crown rot sometimes. That made the violets stand up tall over the brims of the pots, their roots pushing the soil into a hard brown mushroom of dirt and grey filament. Gene thought the violets at their loveliest when taken with crown rot. Sick and beautiful and rotting, they stood up in exotic little crowns, blooming out their last blue and lavender underneath the plain little windows of the doll kitchen in the doll town of Johnsboro.

# Three

In THE QUARTERS every street was named for a Republican president. Beatrice lived on President Lincoln Street. There were no apartments here as in the white part of town, where all streets were named for a Confederate general. Instead each Negro family had a small cottage with three or four rooms to it and a screened porch across the front. The Quarters spread over a high Nantahala hill, behind the smelter, in what was perhaps the most scenic part of Johnsboro. More than one white person, caught by the natural loveliness of the view, the green hill and the sweep of Lake John below with its mother Yadkin stretching in the distance, had wondered "How come the niggers got the best place?"

It was an afterthought. Piedmont Aluminum had drawn the Negroes as flies to a lump of sugar. They could tolerate well the heat of the potrooms and the wages there were the highest paid for unskilled labor anywhere in the state of North Carolina. And so Piedmont Aluminum welcomed the Negroes and built them their cottages and stuck them up behind the smelter on a hill known forever afterwards as the Quarters.

Beatrice had come here with Will Turner when he went to work in the potrooms in about 1923 or so. All their years had left them only one son, Troy Turner, and when he grew up (past child-labor age) he, too, went to work in the potrooms. After Troy grew up, Beatrice had brought her mother, Jancy, to live with her and Will in the Quarters. Jancy was ancient, as old as Eden, and a lot wiser. Beatrice didn't really know how old her mama was. And she had never seen or heard mentioned the name of the man whose issue she herself was. Beatrice had always been plump black Bee-AT-treece, following along behind Jancy and minding, until she married Will Turner and he brought her to live in Johnsboro.

Beatrice tried to tip carefully in to Jancy's bedside. The old woman lay still as a brown mist, her coverlet a spiderwork of faded strips: spangled blues and yellows, a thin patch of green velvet and, pieced right beside it, a patch of overall denim.

"Mama," Bea said, bending close to Jancy's ear. "Mama, I gone now. There a egg and a cake of sausage warming in the oven. And Sunday Jo here to fetch on you."

The old lids fluttered, then opened on a pair of eyes glazed by cataracts. Jancy's skin was pale and honey-hued, webbed by the years that had come silent as spiders and left her with only a tracery of their passing. In her right ear lobe she wore a tiny gold circlet thrust through the soft dim flesh as delicately cruel as a fish barb.

"Get out of this house." Her voice was low and too rich for such a frail body. "I ain't stole nothin. But I mighten cut me somethin with this here knife if you don't move." She raised up an empty hand. It was so thin the sun seemed to filter right through it and make of it an amber carving.

"Mama! It's me! Beatrice! You dreaming, Mama." Beatrice moved back as Jancy suddenly sat up, quick as a bird, and glared at her. "Mama?"

"Shet up," said Jancy. The wool on her skull was whiter than the pillows she had lain upon. In the light, her eyes shone with dull blue iridescence and she squinted impatiently. "Where that no 'count gal at?"

Beatrice hollered over her shoulder, "Sunday, come in here and help Mama Jan to get up."

As the little girl slid in the door past Beatrice's fat belly and hip, Beatrice said again, "I gone now, Mama. Don't get yourself fretted none today. Sunday Jo here. And she better stay here tills I get back."

It was a relief to Bea to get out of the house. Generally, Jancy was good and didn't give them any trouble. But here lately she had taken to mumbling about the old days and dreaming real fierce and just acting downright crazy. Beatrice shook her head and hurried down President Lincoln Street. It was downhill all the way to the cement walk that rounded the smelter and came out on the white side. When she moved, no matter how slight a gesture, Beatrice undulated brown mountains of flesh, ripples and torrents and tides of Negro flesh. But her voice belonged to a skinny woman. It was high-pitched, shrill, and scrawny. At the end of the street, in front of New Resurrection Church, Bea stopped. Seeing Mr. Ledbetter, the mail carrier, trudging along under his heavy satchel, she squawled forth "Good morning, yonder, Mr. Ledbetter. Is you feeling good?" He nodded yes and smiled. "Well, does you have any mail for me?" she bawled again. He nodded no and trudged on.

Men were changing shifts in the potrooms and office clerks were coming for the day. Cars entered and left the parking lots. The men carried black lunch boxes and seemed hurried to get away. This prompted Beatrice to hurry herself on around the fence and across the strip of highway separating Piedmont Aluminum from true Johnsboro. She then made her way through the other streets and finally down a particular alley behind Lee Street. Huffing and gasping, she waddled through the backyard and into the Jim Kulp apartment.

"Bea's here," chimed the twins and then scurried into the living room. Their names were Constance Lucille and Candace Leila, shortened to Connie Lou and Candie Lee, and they were identical.

"Bea! Bea!" cried the twins. "Come see our goldfish we got in Wilby's dime store Saturday."

"Just a minute," panted Beatrice, dropping into a kitchen chair. "I got to set. My heart's racing."

Rose Kulp came in. She was holding some bobby pins between her teeth and scratching around for something in the bottom of her patent leather purse.

"Beatrice," she said through the bobby pins, scarcely moving her lips. "I'm leaving now. This is my week to drive, you know. Jim's already gone to the plant. And I think everything's just about okay here."

She snapped the purse shut, slipped the bobby pins in her reddish-blond hair (the same color as the twins'), kissed each child goodbye, and went out the front door.

Beatrice sniffed to herself as she sat in the apartment and listened to the car motor start up and then the scrunch of gravel and rubber tires. She didn't approve of Mrs. Kulp's working in the mill over at Fairview, a town seven miles to the west of Johnsboro, larger, and also the county seat.

"No white lady with proper raising would work in a mill," said Beatrice, "no matter how poor she got."

But it did matter. And Rose Kulp worked. And if Beatrice had ever stopped to consider the situation, she would have realized that Rose's working was what had kept herself in a job for so long. Beatrice kept the twins all day. They were only five and not yet in school. And even if they had been in school she would still have been there to cook lunch for Jim and to do what housekeeping there was to be done. She had started working for the Kulps after Christa was born and had been with them ever since. Sometimes she even stayed at night if Rose needed her. And sometimes she did a little for other folks up and down Lee Street.

Bea sighed and got up. "I might as well get to washing these dishes." She picked up a plate. The design underneath the egg yellow and bacon grease was "Cattails."

"Look here at this plate!" she hollered at the little girls running around the kitchen, tumbling over each other, their long red braids tangling and coming untied. They stopped and looked at Beatrice.

"You all done waste a egg. Didn't eat half of it." She turned on the water and the soap bubbles rose about her brown hands. "You all the wastefulest white younguns I know of. A person could live off what you all wastes. *Two* persons could!"

"Oh, Bea," they said together, "we ate all we wanted. Besides we don't like eggs."

"Then your mama ought not to fix 'em for you. If you's my younguns"—Beatrice smacked the plate, clean and glistening, the red cattails slick as red bone, into the rubber rack to dry— "if you's my younguns, I'd starve you!"

Candie Lee and Connie Lou stuck out their tongues at Beatrice and then ran away giggling. Christa was coming down the stairs and they stopped running long enough to say, "Bea's been hollering at us. But we don't care. We going out to feed our fishes again." They scampered off to the side porch where their fish swam in a round glass bowl, making lazy golden circles and festooning the water with tiny bubbles.

Christa was ten-going-on-eleven. She looked at herself in the oval mirror that hung over the living-room sofa. The gilt of the frame made her hair seem tenaciously red and she frowned. Mama wanted her to cut her hair. It was thick and the color of new pennies. Her brows and lashes were pale. Her eyes were sometimes grey, sometimes blue, depending on what she wore. And her skin was the kind that freckled profusely in summer. She opened her mouth and looked at the thin wire buckled around her upper teeth. She couldn't remember ever having had teeth without braces on them.

"What you doing?" Bea was standing in the kitchen door, wiping her hands on a dishrag. "I done heard that bell ring two times. And if you don't twist your tail soon, it's gone ring number three and then you gone be tardy. And Miz Benfield say you can't be tardy no more this year."

Christa eyed Bea in the mirror and closed her mouth. She gathered an armful of books off the desk at the end of the sofa and stuck a yellow pencil behind her ear.

"I'm going, Bea, I'm going," she replied lamely and started for the door.

"Wait a minute, youngun. What's the matter with you this morning? Is you sick?" Beatrice was keen to the mood and change in this child. Usually Christa was fiery and ready to argue with her. Bea chided and screeched and threatened, braided her hair so tightly that her eyes watered, and held up her faults before the others. But Christa was her child. And she would easily have sacrificed all the rest of the family to the salvation of this one. Ever since the white child was a toddling baby in diapers, Beatrice and Christa had been both a source of comfort and a source of torment to each other. More than once Rose Kulp had come in from work ready to take the little girl in her lap, only to have the baby run from her and tug and cry at Beatrice's skirt. Rose had missed all the big moments in Christa's life. Like the time she crawled up under the apartment building and wouldn't come out. She sat there, all scrooched up, surrounded by plumbing pipes, old bottles, and mushrooms, and never bothered to answer the pleas of her mother and father. But when Beatrice had stooped over and said, almost breathless from squeezing her formidable abdomen against her kneecaps, "Come on out of there you little idiot!" the child had slithered forth as meekly as if Gabriel himself had sounded the call to Judgment.

This morning, though, she wasn't under the apartment. And she wasn't a baby. She just stood at the partly opened door, fingering the knob, and answered, "I don't know, Bea. I feel okay, I guess."

"Well, *I* guess you needs a spring tonic. Your blood thin or something." Beatrice waited for the child to speak, to reveal. But there was only a silence. The school bell rang.

"Bea, I'm tardy again," said Christa Kulp, and went out the door into Lee Street.

# Four

LINDA EARL GLENN looked at the apartment: so untidy; and at the children: Darryl with peanut butter in both corners of his mouth; Carolyn, wet again, and she'd just changed her not ten minutes ago. Next door she could hear Beatrice squawling at the Kulp twins and clanging pans about in the kitchen. Whenever Bea walked especially heavy, the pictures on Linda Earl's living-room walls trembled dangerously. She went over to straighten them. They were silhouettes, a Marie Antoinette with curls piled high on her head, and a man with lace ruffles at his throat. Her wedding presents.

"Mommie, can I have a Co-Cola?" Darryl stood at her knee, his wide eyes looking ever so much like a pair of chocolate buttons.

"Sure," she said, "and you can take it out in the back if you want to."

"Oh, boy!" The little boy jumped into the kitchen and kept on jumping while she opened the refrigerator and fixed the Coca-Cola. After he had gone outside, Linda Earl wearily changed Carolyn and put her to bed with a bottle of milk. She came back downstairs and plugged in the iron and then pulled it out discontentedly. She didn't want to iron. The clock in the stove said 2:15. A stack of dishes stood in the sink still soiled from lunch. And before her, on the table, sat the peanut butter jar with finger marks all around it and a smeared knife sticking out of the top. Somewhere in the apartment building, in somebody's bathroom, a commode flushed and the plumbing reverberated.

Linda Earl went into the living room and stretched out on the studio couch. She stared up at the ceiling. It was made of beaverboard like the walls. All the interiors of the apartments in Johnsboro were constructed of beaverboard, thin, easy to poke nails through if you were too heavy with the hammer, and extremely conductive of sound. It had a pitted finish. Linda Earl thought it looked like the rind of an orange, except, of course, that it was painted in a dullish dingy cream color. She sighed deeply and put her hands behind her head. And she began again, as she so often had lately, to wander through herself, stumbling into closed doors and falling upon rubble, wiping at cobwebs, trying to feel out her frustration.

"Oh, Michael has it so easy," she thought. "He just goes to work and that's it. I sit and stare and . . . oh, gripes."

She closed her eyes and tried to sleep. But she couldn't keep her eyes shut all the way. The light filtered through and everything seemed red and warm. And a little crackly old-fashioned voice came into her mind and flickered about like a candle inside a jack-o'-lantern. *It don't take long.*

Linda Earl opened her eyes and stared up again. *Granny.* Granny Little had said that. Funny thing. She had not really thought of Granny since the wedding, that hot, sticky, confused wedding. And now she was dead and buried almost two years. Linda Earl thought hard and the pitted orange-peel ceiling seemed to melt apart and take her back to the wedding.

The day she married was a sultry Wednesday in August.

"Marryin in the middle of the week ain't proper," complained Granny Little. "It ought to be on a Saturday, or, bettern that, on a Sunday!"

But nobody paid any attention to her. Linda Earl's mother sent the cousins to the woods to gather bunches of fox ferns and then she set the ferns in crocks along each side of the hall. By three o'clock that afternoon they were all wilted down and the smell was something awful. And then the wedding cake fell because one of the cousins came in and asked Viola a question right when she was measuring flour and afterwards she couldn't remember if she'd already used one cup or two cups. And as if all that wasn't enough, Linda Earl had to go and stick her finger on a hatpin and bleed on her dress.

"Why does it have to be me? Why does everything always have to happen to me? You'd think, just once, just once, things would go my way!"

"Hold still," said Mother, dabbing at the blood spot with a cold rag. "This ought to blanch it out. Blood always is the hatefulest stuff to try to work out."

Granny Little was sitting in the corner, rocking hard, her arms clasped tightly around her thin shoulders. She always sat that way.

"The day I'se married was a cold day in Jan-yee-ary. Snow piled high each side the door. My ma was fit to tie. 'Fraid the preacher wouldn't make it. He had to come five mile or more." She cackled. Every time Granny laughed, the sounds of it broke about her into sharp little pieces of glass and tin.

"Wouldn't of been no scandal if he hadn't made it, would there, Granny?" Mother giggled, glancing up from Linda Earl's skirt.

Granny Little straightened in her chair and looked out the window at the grain fields waving in the sun.

"I'll affirm, if they don't take off more and more of that yard every year in that wheat field."

She turned back. "Naw. It 'uz eight years 'fore Tom come. Wan't no scandal there."

She smiled a secret little faraway smile, looking back around at the fields and beyond them at the intensely blue sky.

"Preacher made it all right. The hoss a-flounderin through all that snow. He made it and I'se married good and proper with Ma and all 'em lookin on. Me and Albert Little. And we went away in the snow to his little bitty old house. Wan't nothin but a cabin. We called it the Little's littlest house. But he laid on a big fire. Albert could always make the biggest fire, out of just piddling wood, of any man I ever knowed."

Linda Earl shifted impatiently. "Don't you have that spot out yet, Mother?"

Brushing back a wisp of hair from her eyes, Mother stood up and laid the rag on the bureau in front of Linda Earl.

"I reckon that'll have to do. Ain't all out. But it'll have to do. Besides that, we going to keep the shades drawed down in the parlor while the wedding's going on. Won't nobody notice it."

Linda Earl turned around carefully in front of the bureau glass. She was young, only eighteen, and lovely in a doll-like way. Her beauty was the kind that could too easily turn into monotony: a round smooth face with no distinguishing marks except a dimple in each cheek when she smiled right; brown eyes; lips that looked pretty under paint; and long brown hair fluffed out in curls. She was a doll to sit on top a little girl's bed, one of those called boudoir dolls. And that's exactly what she'd been all her life, a doll, and now she was a bride doll. The wedding dress was made of some kind of sleek shimmering material, not satin though. Mother had gotten it on sale in Fairview. It fell in long soft folds to the tops of her slippers. She wore a piece of white veil upon her head and, after carefully removing every thorn, had tied up a bouquet of roses to carry in her arms. She studied herself, every curve, every curl, even opening her mouth to examine her teeth. After a while she stood hand on hip and said to herself in the mirror, "I look good and I know I do."

Granny Little turned back again from the window.

"What you going do with that dress after you's married?"

Linda Earl looked around, the piece of veil moving in a little fluttering of snowflakes over her hair.

"What do you mean *what'm I going to do with it?*" She tried to say it flippantly, but something inside her started to get uneasy.

Granny Little sat rocking and grinning at Linda Earl. Behind her the sultry August air shimmered in the window, making a little blue halo for her head.

"Now, Granny," started Mother, "let's don't get in none of your quarrels. It's so hot and the youngun's been flustered enough already!"

She shook out the folds of Linda Earl's dress and stood back to view the girl. Satisfied with the dress and the blanched-out spot, she went to the bedroom door and, with one back look at Linda Earl and then at the old woman, said, "You'd best be gettin into the parlor, now, Granny. Most of the folks is just about here. I'll send one of the boys in to help you."

After she had gone, the two continued to look at one another across the room and soon Linda Earl tried to be flippant again and to ask again, "Just what do you mean, Granny? I don't understand."

The little old woman in the chair just grinned and rocked. Her eyes sparkled, the same deep brown as the girl's, but bred out of more sense, more vision, more hurt.

Linda Earl was getting impatient.

"Well!" she snapped.

"Well!" answered Granny Little. "*I'll* tell you, since *you* can't tell me. You going stand up here this afternoon in front of these fine people. And you going to say 'yes' this and 'I do'

that and you ain't going know one word you's sayin, much less
what it means. Then you going over yonder to Johnsboro with
that Michael Glenn, who don't look any more like a man than
you do a woman, and you going live in a pasteboard box and
you going hang this dress in your closet. After a while you
going cut the tail offen it and wear it for Sunday best. 'Fore
long, it going be next-to-Sunday-best. Then it going get cut
up for collars and facings. And it finally going end up being
drug through the yard by the younguns!"

She paused to shift her shrunken old body in the rocking
chair and to take a deep breath. But before she could say more,
one of the cousins came in and took her away. And Linda Earl
was left standing before the mirror in a white dress and a white
veil, holding an armful of white roses, and set on fire by a
mind, which heretofore had been about as white and blank as
the dress, but which was now flaming in color.

Needles and pins began to prick Linda Earl's arms, so she
took them out from under her head and sat up on the couch.
As she rubbed her blood back into circulation, she was struck
all at once by a peculiar thought. Linda Earl, perhaps, did not
really appreciate how peculiar or reflective it was. But she
remembered having seen a book at school once, on somebody's
desk top. It was called *The Decline and Fall of the Roman
Empire*. And on the cover were three marble columns. The
first was complete, perfect, with a top of little curly leaves and
scrolls. The second was broken in two, the curly top gone, just
a broken white shaft. And the third one was only a crumble of
white stones. And now as she thought of it, Granny Little's
words had been exactly like those three columns on the book
cover. First you're going to hang this dress up in a closet.
Then it's going to get cut off for a second-best dress. And
finally it is drug around by the children through the dirt, nothing but a ruin any more. Boom, boom, boom. Once, two, three,

and you're out. All this was giving Linda Earl a headache, so she got up and went into the kitchen for an aspirin and a glass of water. She chewed the little sour crumbs (she could never swallow aspirins for gagging) and looked out the back door at Darryl. He was playing soldier, running and then falling on his stomach in mock agony, then jumping up and sneaking around behind trees, then falling again.

"How can he die so much?" she thought. The water was cool and she decided to fix a big glass with ice and go out in the back with Darryl. But as she stood at the screen door, Granny Little came back again, that day, that hour; all of it passed through her mind like the sound of an old-fashioned player piano grinding away in some Victorian parlor.

All through the ceremony, Granny had sat proud as a queen in Mother's brocaded wing chair and the candlelight had softened her wrinkled old face. Then it was over and Miss Campbell, that music teacher of her childhood, had played loudly and there'd been cake and punch in the dining room. Mother turned on the chandelier she was so proud of (it had electric bulbs instead of candles) and everyone had been gay, sipping at their punch cups and clapping Michael on the back. But later, outside, it was different. She and Michael, married, flushed with the heat of the day, were getting into the car. Granny had insisted that she be allowed to watch the going-off. And just before Linda Earl closed the door of the car, the old woman had put a hand on her arm. She leaned over, her poor eyes so blinded in the sun that she appeared to be weeping, and she whispered in a broken crackling whisper, "It don't take long, honey. Be a good one, if you can." And so they drove off in a hail of old shoes and rattling cans, JUST MARRIED scrawled all over Michael's car in crumbling soap.

*It don't take long.* Well, it didn't take long to find out that getting married was not just getting dressed up in a white gown and carrying flowers. You couldn't go on putting on that dress every day and getting married over and over in Mother's parlor, having folks admire you, giving you presents, and saying what a pretty bride you made.

Linda Earl frowned and shook her head. The headache was going to come back if she didn't stop. She decided to think about Michael. But no, thinking of Michael didn't help any more. It would bring on another siege of worrying. A fly buzzed against the screen. Out in the grass, Darryl died and was resurrected over and over. Linda Earl Glenn opened the door and went down the steps to the glider. She had put all thoughts out of her mind now. She would not think at all. She would be clean and white and blank. And when Michael came home maybe he would wash the dishes for her.

# Five

"Need anything else, son?" Doc Tracey held the little
white paper bag over the counter.

"No, not this time." Gene took the bag and then nodded to
Doc and the old druggist smiled and nodded back. It was a
polite way of saying "Put this on the bill." Doc Tracey
shuffled back to his dispensary behind the soda counter and
little booths where mirrors reflected endlessly the images of a
patient old man in a white smock mixing and pouring and
stoppering.

It was a hot day for spring and overhead the old-fashioned
black fans, suspended from the ceiling on black cords, swung
their long blades fiercely. Everything in the drugstore seemed
old-fashioned and dark, but also very cool and restful and almost timeless. There was no chromium or plastic or neon; only
marble and glass and the swoosh of the fans hovering above
like gigantic beetles.

Outside the heat bristled up with all the irritability of a dog
disturbed at rest. Gene stuffed the paper bag, Elizabeth's medi-
cine, the Stami-Cine, in his pocket and walked along. Kids
were going home from school, slitting the heavy afternoon air
with their noise and scattering the streets with pieces of blue-

lined paper that bore black scraggly letters. He liked to be inside the drugstore. It reminded him of Rebecca, cool and dark, with the rich gleam of the marble-topped counter. That marble brought still another sensation, equally pleasant, the taste of mint. When he was a child and had visited his kin in Virginia, the Negro cook made mints for him. After boiling and stirring in a huge kettle, she poured the syrup out on a slab of marble and carefully dropped a tincture of mint oil into it. Then, while Gene watched, she worked the hot candy into a long skein and pulled and pulled until the stuff was like silk in her hands. Slowly the clearness deepened into creamy white and when she had finished a rope of mint lay across the kitchen table.

That whiteness, the smell of hot syrup and mint oil, the touch of the marble, Rebecca in the snow. Gene stumbled on the curb and looked around nervously to see if anyone had caught him in so vulnerable an occupation as daydreaming.

"Stupid ass," he scolded himself, but continued to dream on across the street and down the back alleys. Rebecca was probably a nurse by now, in cap and apron, maybe wearing a gauze mask. Gene dreamed of himself ill, fevered and broken, wounded, lying on a cot. And Rebecca came winding bandages over his body, soothing, kissing, a needle, the flash of knives, pain, and the sweet darkness of death.

"I wonder if I'd really trust her to nurse me?" It was one thing to lie naked and helpless on a bed before strangers and quite another to lie throbbing under the impersonal touch of the Adored One. "Oh, good God!" he said, now morose and angry with himself, kicking the blue gravels of the alley. Everything seemed gone wrong in his world. He tried to think back and remember a time when he had ever been truly happy. Maybe in the Virginia kitchen, with Aunty Wincey and the mints? No. He wanted to blame someone, so he decided to blame Elizabeth. *Mother*. He sneered at the word and then was immediately sorry. Poor Elizabeth, wilting away in this place, just like her damned African violets. There was the ore dust from the smelter. It drifted all over the town of Johnsboro, sifting in through screens and settling along the porch railings and on the floor, a grey powdery film, gun-metal grey. Ore dust gave Elizabeth the asthma.

"I might just as well be buried!" she complained to Edward Boyette, wheezing all the while and coughing daintily into a little handkerchief. "You brush it away, but it comes right back with the next wind."

And when the asthma was gone, the bad headaches would come. And then a weak spell. And the Stami-Cine. Gene wondered what they really did for her, the little red pills that she so diligently swallowed, following each one with a sip of water from a long-stemmed crystal goblet on her night table. *God*, it must take tremendous love for fellow man to nurse sick people. Like Rebecca Byrd did. Gene could only feel annoyance. Maybe they weren't all like Elizabeth, though. And the exasperating thing about her was that she never raised her voice, even when complaining, she never even made a sour face or pouted. She was so damned sweet about it. How could you get mad at her?

It seemed that all his life, Gene Boyette had been trying to get mad at Elizabeth, his mother. Or to make her get mad at him. Then he would know the mark, the boundary, the place that stood between her and him. Then he would know that he existed, that his will could be felt. It never had worked. When he was four, he went into her closet and looked at all the garments hanging primly on their hangers, at the rows of shoes, their toes all pointed, perfectly matched and polished, the handbags on the shelf, the ruffly gowns she wore in bed, and the fur cape she wore to church. He looked and he looked and he felt the anger seethe and hiss and spill out of him. The door opened, a wedge of light split his swoon and he stepped out.

"What are you doing?" she asked without the faintest tremor of anxiety in her voice.

"I'm making spit," he answered. "I spit on your dress, I spit on your new shoes, I spit on your fur. I'm making spit."

He waited for the first signs of vexation, a quivering, a cry, a wagging finger. None appeared. Elizabeth could not lose self-control. "Oh," she said weakly, "you are a naughty boy." And then she went to bed, swaddled in a mauve coverlet, leaving a note to Edward that she would not be down to dinner.

Gene paused for a moment. He had reached Stuart Street. His father's apartment stood alone from the others. It was an end-apartment in what had been a row of four. The others had caught fire once, long before the Boyettes came to Johnsboro from Virginia, and they had burned to the ground. Only the end one was saved and now it stood along the corner of Stuart Street with a patch of grass on each side and a mass of shiny ivy growing up the side where the other apartments had once been attached. It was really quite attractive. And its aloofness was something Elizabeth Boyette earnestly maintained. She wasn't exactly snobby, but the people of Stuart Street felt the distance between them and her. Edward got along fine with the men at the smelter. He was a metallurgist, a graduate of V.P.I., and genuinely sociable. But Elizabeth couldn't help herself. She had been born into blue blood, not money, but blue blood, the kind that measures itself in family trees and polite little afternoon visits and the number of sons at William and Mary. She really disliked the people of Johnsboro with their easy friendliness and their big smiles. Edward often said to her why not build a house somewhere, in Johnsboro or in the country outside. But Elizabeth had her eyes and mind back in

Virginia. And for her only child and son, Edward Eugene Boyette, Junior, she had chosen a return to that blue blood of her girlhood. Already she had written for brochures from William and Mary. "It's such a nice old school and Williamsburg is such a fine old town." How she would have shuddered had she known that her son had fallen in love with a girl of Johnsboro, North Carolina, a girl whose father had worked all his life as a foreman in the potrooms and died of pneumonia contracted while sitting outside all night in the dead of winter, drunk, singing like a sparrow at the gate of paradise. A girl whose mother smoked Lucky Strike cigarettes right down to the quick and cursed at people over the telephone and was an Unbeliever. And that wasn't all. Edward Eugene Boyette, Junior, had fallen in love with something else. Or maybe the truth of it was that he had fallen out of love. In any case, the time stood right for a change.

He confronted them at dinner. The Boyettes had a dining room, something unusual in the apartments of Johnsboro where the kitchen served as a dining room and everyone sat and ate and looked into the sink at all the dirty pots and pans. But this was really an addition, made after the fire that left their apartment a house unto itself. And they had Alice, a young Negro girl who tended the table and waited on Elizabeth during her weak spells. Alice was quiet and placid, not like the loud garrulous Bea that belonged to the Jim Kulps. Alice was pouring the coffee. Gene looked directly across the table at Elizabeth and said, "I am going in the Navy," and then took a bit of pie. It was dewberry. His least favorite. And somehow this insignificant fact made him more certain of his decision and gave him great strength to announce it.

Elizabeth could not turn pale because she was always pale; even in her healthiest moments she was of a pallor, not ivory or porcelain, but of the death-white satin that lines a coffin.

"What!" She sat very stiff in her chair, her silver spoon immobile in a little pocket of air just above the rim of her cup. Edward, too, had stopped eating and was looking intently upon him. So Gene said again, "I am going in the Navy."

"But you can't! You're too young. And you're going to college after graduation. To William and Mary. It's all arranged!"

"When did you decide all this, son?" Edward's voice was very calm. He had already concluded, in just the few moments, that his son's decision was all right, perhaps a bit romantic, but all right. He began to eat again.

"Today. Oh, not *today*. I talked with the recruiting officers a long time ago, back in the winter, at Fairview one Saturday. They were pretty keen on a guy having a high-school education and all that to start with. . . ."

"A high-school education! But a *college* education is what you want. Is what *I* want!"

"Elizabeth, I can get that in the Navy, too, if I want it." Gene turned away from her and began to talk exclusively to his father. "There's a lot of papers and stuff to get signed and a physical. And I'll need your consent."

"I won't consent."

She pushed back her chair and stood up; her face for once was not pale, but extremely red and her lips began to tremble. Her carefully arched eyebrows (she spent hours with a tiny gold-backed mirror and pair of tweezers) rose in twin crescents. She looked first at her husband and then at her son.

"I will not consent. Edward? Eugene? Never." And then she burst into tears.

Edward got up immediately and began to console her. Gene continued to eat, crunching the little dewberry seeds, detesting each one for the unpleasant feeling in his mouth, yet pleased with his unpleasantness because of its strange strength. Alice came round to his place and he moved slightly in order that she could more easily pour the coffee. During all this she had not spoken a word or made a sign that she even heard it. Gene fastened his mind on Alice. She was very light-skinned and slender and her black hair was almost Indian-straight, held in place by a narrow green ribbon. A few more bleachings and Alice could pass for white. Alice moved shadow-quiet, carrying the silver coffeepot like a brace of lighted candles before her back into the kitchen and softly closed the door. She was infinitely more graceful than was Elizabeth.

Poor Elizabeth. She was protesting again. And his father was speaking.

"Well, we'll settle this thing later, son. Don't make any more plans for right now. I just want to talk to you some more about it all." Then he turned back to Elizabeth, still weeping and beginning to wheeze. Another asthmatic attack.

When it was later, Edward Boyette did talk to his son. And it was settled. Gene went again to Fairview to see the Navy recruiters. It was decided. Elizabeth sat in the audience at his high-school graduation, her face like white stone, her eyes flickering only faintly during the strains of the Recessional. Throughout the early summer they waited for his orders. And in mid-July, he went to Salisbury and boarded a train for Raleigh and from there on to Norfolk, Virginia. Not Williamsburg. In October, he sailed for the Pacific.

Other people's sons could go out and dig foxholes and get shot down in airplanes and drown in the ocean. But Elizabeth Boyette felt her son was totally wasted. What good would he be to her dead? Just a name in bronze upon a silly monument, a miniature flag on an obscure grave. She kept on protesting. She watered the African violets and coughed up ore dust and lay in a darkened bedroom with Stami-Cine at her side. But all her protestings and seizures and certainly none of her fine plans could bring him back or change his mind. He didn't give a good goddamn about his blue blood. It was sure to show up red if spilled. She decided to take a pet. It was a Mexican hairless, purebred, ill-tempered, and devoted to his mistress. She called him Pablo, which means "little one."

## Six

SUMMER CAME to Johnsboro in spite of the war. The obelia bushes blossomed profusely, showering the streets and steps with delicate white flowerlets. And school was out. So Beatrice Turner sometimes brought Sunday Jo to Lee Street. Sunday Jo was Bea's niece, the child of Will Turner's sister, a sister who lived in Detroit, Michigan, and was not married and couldn't keep Sunday Jo and work, too. Sunday was plumpish brown, with a million little pigtails, each one licorice-twisted and bound at the end with a thread. Perspiration beaded her thick top lip.

When Beatrice wasn't looking, they crawled through the upstairs windows onto the porch roof. There was much to view from up here in good weather. Below them little Lee Street ran down and emptied itself, thick with tar and white gravel, into the cement highway at one end and into the hard-packed dust of the schoolyard at the other. The schoolhouse was long and low with a fading white belfry on top. A belfry whose hidden bell tolled thrice each day during school season and whose deep tone could be heard in every corner of Johnsboro. It was summer silent, except for pigeons roosting in the lattices. They made a cooing, pouting sound, the sound of someone blowing bubbles underwater.

Directly behind Lee Street, beyond the gravelly back alley, rose the massive red walls of the Theater. It sat in the middle of downtown Johnsboro like a baroque ornament fashioned of brick and mortar, embellished by cornices, buttresses, Spanish tile, swooping red colonnades, reflecting the sun out front in its barrage of glass doors.

It was really an opera house and the interior was equipped with several heavy chandeliers, an orchestra pit, and tiers of dressing rooms that rose up to the very edges of the roof behind the tremendous and empty stage. It was the oddity of Johnsboro, completely out of element, and sat like a Sphinx, obdurate and indifferent to the apartments clustered about it. But the people of Johnsboro had found a use for it after the occasional touring companies had ceased to come and the local drama groups petered out: the show, always a double-feature plus cartoon on Saturday night.

And since the war another use had been found for it. On top, in huge white letters, was painted JOHNSBORO, N.C., and a big arrow pointed the direction north.

Away in the farthest rim of vision bloomed the smokestacks and buildings of Piedmont Aluminum. There was always a noise in Johnsboro, a kind of hum or buzz emanating from the smelter. People were just used to it, as they were used to the ore dust.

"We going to tell Bea!"

The twins stuck their heads through the window and gawked at Christa and Sunday, jealous that they weren't brave enough to defy Beatrice and get out there on the forbidden roof, too.

"Oh, shut up. You aren't going to do any such of a thing."

Christa crawled back to the window and Sun followed. "Look at all the bird shit out there!" The little girls inside tittered and threatened again. "Whoo! We *are* going to tell Bea. She'll skin you both!"

"If she skins us, then we skin you next." Christa climbed through and brushed the ore dust off her knees. Sunday came in; her brown chubby knees were streaked with grey and white.

The four trooped downstairs and into the kitchen where Bea bustled about getting ready to cook the lunch.

"What you all want? Get out of my nice clean kitchen!" Bea looked up from a pan of biscuits she was starting to push into the oven.

"We don't want nothing but a Popsicle."

They got the Popsicles out of the refrigerator, in the top part where the ice trays were. It needed defrosting, a chore that Beatrice hated more than anything else and one that she usually left till the very last. Thus, the whole compartment was swollen and bearded with heavy white frost.

They went out on the side porch. Christa and Sunday Jo sat in the swing and Candie and Connie flopped down on their stomachs on the porch floor near the screen door. Everyone sucked and licked and stared at nothing in particular. The melted orange syrup dripped on their hands and down their chins onto the floor. A single fly began to travel the bright drops and soon he was joined by another and then these two became a hubbub of glistening wings and orange specklets. And Sunday Jo began to converse upon her favorite subject: witches and spirits and things that walked about in the dead of the night.

"Lucille Haas's ma seen a spirit walk once. It walk in the house plumb across the floor and right past her own bed."

"What did she do?"

"She don't do nothin! She just lay there and watch it, prayin for dear life it don't see her layin there in that bed. It walk up to the meer and fade on through, just like a shadder."

"What happened then?"

Sunday let it steep a bit for effect, glancing around at all of them, then she continued.

"Lucille Haas's ma she just about go crazy right there on the spot, shakin and quiverin and chawin on her tongue. She ain't never been exactly right since. Some says she can't stand meers or store windows or even folks that wears spectickles. Yes, sir, I guess she about crazy."

"Did the police come to shoot her like a mad dog?" This was the twins asking.

"Naw! Course not! She just set in her room all the time and don't bother nobody much."

"Last year Mr. Stanley's dog went crazy. You know that old bird dog he had? And the police came and shot him, right out there in the lot. We seen it, too."

The smell of frying came out of the kitchen. And along with it, the sound of Beatrice's high shrill voice singing "Rescue the Perishing." It was the sound of broken teakettles, of tubercular clarinets, whistling and whining in ecstasy.

Christa wondered how Sunday Jo knew so much. She breathed upon her Popsicle and a little frost vapor rose up tickling her nose and lip. Sunday saved the Popsicle bags to win a bicycle or something. Maybe it was a trip to New York City. Anyhow, she saved all the covers off of Blue Horse tablets, too. Christa had never saved anything except prune-juice bottles. They were short and round and of the darkest green, not emerald or jade, but a deep drowned fathoms-below-sunlight green. Beatrice said once, to persuade the children to drink prune juice, that they were bottles of wine. Christa knew, of course, that Bea was lying. But the first taste of the juice, though brown and only faintly wrought with spice, had seemed at that moment exactly how wine should taste. Wine from a goatskin bag, sweetened in the sun and picked by brown peasant hands. So she had collected all the empty green bottles and then planted them in a sunken little row along the iris beds in the back yard.

Sunday Jo was talking again, sucking loudly upon the orange ice in between her sentences and pumping the swing furiously with one bare brown foot.

"One time Joe Duke and a bunch of them went in Cody Town cemetery and hollered 'All the dead come forth!' as loud as thunder. They hollered it out three times and ain't nothin happened yet. Then old Joe he think he be smart and go right to the middle of the graves, stands on one, and hollers out real loud 'ALL THE DEAD COME FORTH!' Then you know what happened?"

"No, what?"

"Old man Billy Byrd, he was still livin then. You 'members old man Byrd? Always drunk as a coot and six times as ugly? Well, he been passed out long ago right behind the very gravestone where Joe standing. Well, all that hollering and carrying-on done woke him up and he raises up over that gravestone and say, 'I'm a coming Lordy, Lordy. But don't hurry me so!' "

Sunday Jo dissolved into a fit of giggling.

"And then you know what else happened? When old man Byrd found out it won't nothin but Joe Duke and them pesky boys, he was so mad he jump out and pick up Joe by his left ear. Just pick him plumb up off the ground! By his ear!"

Sunday Jo was so tickled that she could not go on another word. The swing shook with laughter.

"Then what? Then *what?*" Christa was giggling herself and pulling Sunday's plump shoulder. Candie and Connie jumped up and down, their faces orange and grinning like jack-o'-lanterns. "What! What!"

Sunday could barely gasp over a whisper.

"Old Joe so scared, he pee all over hisself!"

Beatrice burst through the door. All the children were limp

with laughing. Christa and Sunday Jo sprawled in the swing
and the twins rolled about on the floor, scattering the flies.

"You all get in here and help me cap some berries. You ain't
done nothin all day long but cut the fool. I want to get these
things finished by the time Miz Rose get home this evening.
Now come on!"

Christa and Sunday got up and followed Bea into the house.
Candace Leila and Constance Lucille hopped up also and
peered through the screen into the dark cool interior of the
living room. "We going help you, too, Bea."

"No you ain't. You all won't do nothin but make a mess!"

The twins frowned and pulled down their lower eyelids and
batted their eyes at Bea.

"Get out of here!" Bea swatted at the door and off they
darted. "Big fatsy Bea," they chanted over their shoulders.
"Big fatsy Bea! She has to use a barrel to wee!"

Sunday Jo was most learned on witches.

"Witches I always knows almost on sight," she said solemnly
to Christa as they sat at the kitchen table capping berries.

"They usually don't take a human shape, though. They usually hides inside a spider or a snake or a toad-frog. But sometimes they gets inside a person and makes 'em do their will."

"Humph! Ain't no such of things as witches, gal," sniffed
Beatrice from the sink.

"They is, too! One of 'em killed my real daddy. I know
'cause I seen it!"

"Now where you hear such as that! Your daddy's killed in a
car wreck and you won't even born yet."

Sunday wilted down in her chair, sticking out her lower lip.
Then she suddenly puffed back up like a little brown toad and
cried, "You just jealous 'cause you ain't never seen 'em! You
ask Mama Jan! She seen 'em! She call 'em if she wants. And I
helps 'er!"

Beatrice spun around and shook a fat finger at Sunday. It was soft and pink underneath and dripping with water from the sink.

"Mama Jan don't know nothin about witches or spirits or anything like that! Ain't I taught you bettern that? Don't I take you to New Resurrection Church every week that comes? Ain't you ever listened to a thing the preacher said in there? One of these days the Lord Hisself going strike you dead! And you ain't got no business setting in this kitchen stuffin that white youngun's head full of such trash. Now shetcha mouth and cap them berries!"

Bea turned back to the sink and jerked the spigot on full force. The red berries swam round and round in a big tin pan. She kept on grumbling. "I find live folks enough trouble to contend with without having to worry over the dead 'uns!"

Sunday Jo bent her kinky head over the strawberries and began stripping off the green stems and sepals. But she glanced up through her eyelashes at Christa across the table and the look she sent through the now still, quiet, and steamy kitchen was more than enough to erase Beatrice's harsh diatribe.

Later, when Jim Kulp came in for lunch, they all sat at the table crowned by Beatrice at one end dishing up food like she was chopping weeds with a dull hoe. There were such plain wholesome smells, of pork chop and biscuit, and the darkish fecund smell of Beatrice and Sunday Jo, and the fragile smell of a glass of tuberoses shrinking on the cupboard. Witches seemed awfully out of place and impossible. Christa sat and picked at the embroidery on the edge of the tablecloth. The right side had a design of flowers in May baskets with bluebirds on either side. The underside was a mass of knots and webs, senseless, crazy, mad as a mad dog. Mr. Stanley's poor old bird dog shot by the police as he stood jerking over his water dish. There were so many little threads, so many useless little strands, knots and garlands and clusters of broken color upon a white prairie, a tableland of purest innocence bordered by flamboyant madness.

"I swear to God Hisself, Mr. Jim," said Bea wearily, pausing to wipe her glistening face upon her apron, "if I don't believe the Devil fire his furnace smack up under this kitchen!"

The afternoon whistles blew stridently while they were stacking up the dishes. Mr. Stanley's other bird dogs, the normal ones with placid dog brains, started howling as they always did at the sound of the whistles. Jim went back to work. And all the rest of the day, Beatrice made strawberry jam, filling the apartment with the sweet stifling smell of boiling fruit. At the end of the afternoon, the jam jars sat in a row in the cupboards, red and rich, with a layer of white paraffin on the top. Beatrice put on her hat, took up an armful of assorted paper sacks and the newspaper, and pulling Sunday Jo out the door behind her, said to Christa, "Now you keep them younguns out of my jam. And tell Miz Rose it all done but don't set it in no draft or it'll crack."

And then they left. The apartment seemed terribly dull and safe. Not at all the nest for witches and terror that it had been with Sunday there to adorn it. Christa wandered out onto the porch again. There, high on a wooden table, sat the bowl of fish. The late-afternoon sun shining through the screen fell through the glass walls of the bowl and made of it a glowing chalice. The tiny fish swam round, their eyes dull and unseeing, their fins like webs of filigree. Christa stood and tapped gently upon the bowl. And then she whistled. But the fish could not hear, or see, or speak. If a witch possessed their bodies, she was a witch of silence, golden and impenetrable.

# Seven

J ANCY SAT on the porch dozing. Every now and then a fly lit on her arm or on her leg and she would swat at it without ever opening her eyes. Outside her grandson Troy Turner was building a fire to fry fish. He'd just brought a mess of them back from Lake John. Every summer the water receded and this summer it had receded more than ever. Whole stretches of lake bottom lay bare to the sun. Big old carp and catfish got trapped in the backwash pools. Jancy heard Troy telling some-body on the street, "The water was just a-workin with them things. You oughta of seen it! A man could just stand there and scoop 'em up. Just scoop 'em up!"

She chuckled to herself and dozed off again, this time to those distant wild summers of long ago when the sun rolled and burned out of the southern sky and there wasn't any Lake John. She was just a slip of a girl, maybe twelve or thirteen years, but already the men had been casting their eyes on her. On that pretty skin of hers. That honey-golden skin that stretched itself so smoothly over her small bones and flowering breasts. Jancy smiled and nodded her old cotton-white head, so pleased with the image of herself of long ago, barefoot, patting down the road in a yellow print skirt and no bodice, going fishing with the Young Doctor. He was something, the Young Doctor Jim.

"Hope nobody don't decide to have no babies this afternoon, Jancy," he'd laugh. "If they do, Pa'll have to bring 'em for us. You didn't tell, did you, Jan?"

Pa was the Old Doctor Jim. Doctor James Westbrook and Doctor James Westbrook, Junior. The Young Doctor Jim wasn't married, but there were plenty out to get him.

When they got to the river (it was the real honest-to-God river, not any piddling Lake John) he tied a cord around a jug and let it down in the water. The other end he fastened to a clump of bushes growing on the bank. Then while she, Jancy, scratched around in the damp red earth for some worms to bait their hooks, the Young Doctor Jim would settle back against a tree, light up his long cigar, and start out on the women.

"Jancy," he'd say, taking a deep puff, the cigar glowing like a little red cat eye, "now that Avery woman is a heaven to behold. I'll swear if she ain't. Blond hair a-hanging plumb down to her ass, eyes just as big and blue as God's own angels', and a pair of paps that'd make a bulldog break his chain. Lord God!" He shut his eyes in mock rapture.

Jancy stuck two fat worms on the hooks and threw out both lines, anchoring the poles under a big rock. Then she perched on the rock and sat very still, listening to the Young Doctor.

"But she ain't the one for me, Jancy. Naw siree."

"How come that, Doctor Jim?" Jancy didn't really care, but the white man liked to talk, so she let him talk. She was good at listening.

"Ain't no *woman* to her. She's got the tits and she's got the face. But she don't know she's got 'em. That woman's got a problem she don't know about. It's 'Now, Doctor Westbrook, we're having our Quarterly Missionary Meeting this next Sunday evening and I'm wondering if maybe you'd be so kind as to render us a little program.' Or 'My dear Doctor Westbrook, being as you are such a fine upstanding member of our community, I do wish you'd speak to our young people and warn them against the evils of strong drink and dalliance.' I can imagine her sex organs are made out of porcelain and probably about as responsive." He straightened and asked, "You 'spect that jug's cold yet, honey?" And, as Jancy fetched it, said again, "No, Virginia Avery ain't for me. She might do for a preacher or maybe even Jesus Christ Hisself. But not for old James Westbrook, M.D."

He unstoppered the jug and took a long drink. "Ah." He leaned back with his eyes half-shut. "Nothin like the good old corn. Have one, Jan, but swallow easy."

Jancy lifted the jug to her lips and sipped one little swallow. It was cold from the river, but the taste was hot as fire. Tears came to her eyes and her nose tingled. She felt the liquor travel downwards and spread the flaming petals of a sunflower through her veins. Doctor Jim continued.

"Now Lou May is a different story. Right the other way. Good old Lou May Harkness. Full of the urge from the day she's born. All a man has to do is look at her twice and she spreads." He threw back his head and laughed; the green canopy over them shivered as the birds set up a scolding and squirrels jumped along the branches. "But there's one thing about old Lou May, though, that makes her bettern most."

"What's that?" Jancy slapped at a mosquito on her thigh. Two tiny hard lumps appeared and she bent her mouth to suck at them.

"She don't make any pretense at being what she ain't. I love her for that, Jancy, I swear I do. But I still couldn't marry that one."

"Who *is* you going marry, Doctor Jim? The Old Doctor done say if you don't marry by the year he goin cut you off."

"I know." The Young Doctor Westbrook, Jr., sighed and drew at his cigar, "I know."

He became silent and distant and sat so solemnly still that it seemed the only living thing about him was the tiny glow of the ember in his cigar. Jancy got up to check the poles. There was nothing. Both hooks dangled empty.

"Somethin got them worms," she muttered and proceeded to bait them once more. After setting the poles again, she waded out. The river was cold. It was always cold, but there would be one thin patch of warm ripples way out in the middle where the sun beat down untrammeled by branch or leaf. But along the bank the vines and bushes kept everything shady. And it was there the brown water bubbled chill across Jancy's feet.

"Hey, Jan!" hollered the Young Doctor after a while. "You better not get out yonder in that river too far. Might step in a hole over your head and where would I be then without no little nigger to talk to and fetch my likker and catch my fish?"

Jancy giggled and waded back to shore. "You could get some of them highfalutin white women to wait on you, Doctor."

One of the corks bobbed and dipped under. Jancy scrambled over and jerked it up. Another empty hook swung glistening in the air. She cast it down sulkily and said, "You is the worst fish luck I ever seen, Doctor Jim. I never catch no fish when I comes with you!"

"Nobody but an idiot goes fishing to catch fish, Jancy."

Something in his voice made her turn sharply. He was still just sitting and leaning against the tree, drawing at the cigar, but there was a wistful faraway look in his eyes. The look of a child who clings to his rag doll and tries to look bravely out the door into the yard where his brothers are playing at war.

They walked back in silence at the end of the afternoon: the Young Doctor with his jug demurely cloaked in a black leather satchel; and Jancy following along dragging the poles in the dust behind her. At the fork of the road, where one part went on to Westbrook and the other down to the cabins, Doctor Jim stopped and leaned over close and peered into Jancy's eyes and said, "Can you keep a secret, little nigger?"

His breath was rotten with corn liquor and his cheeks were all flushed. But Jancy, delighted, laughed and answered, "Course! What is it?"

Doctor Jim paused a few moments, peering at her intently, then he said, "Her name's Rachael. And she is *beautiful and well-favored.*" Then he stood tall against the evening sky and laughed louder than ever. "Rachael!" he shouted.

Jancy stirred from her dreaming and looked around. Out in the yard, Troy's fire crackled and popped, the orange flames jumping through a small grill laid between bricks.

" 'Bout time for Bea to get home. I do hope she bring me somethin. Bring me a little present or somethin." The old head fell again and the eyelids, thin and delicate as pieces of golden filigree, slipped shut. It was such a long time, so many years, so many wars, but the freshness of those days could come back as fast as the scent of the hyacinths in Miss Rachael's wedding bouquet.

Doctor Jim said, "Here's the prettiest little nigger in the whole world." Then Doctor Jim went off with the Palmer Regiment and he only came back once before he was killed. And he said to Jancy, "You take good care of my woman till I get back and I'll give you freedom." And Jancy agreed and gave Doctor Jim her solemn sworn word. Then there was the flare of a lantern and the sound of hoofs on the road and the thump of her heart inside her. And they saw him no more.

All the other niggers ran off, shouting "Jubilee" and ca-pering, grinning like black fools in paradise. But she, little old yellow Jancy, stayed right by Miss Rachael like she'd promised. And together they rooted and scratched enough out of the ground to keep alive. At night, while she sliced apples to dry on the roof or cut little shirts and gowns out of all the scraps she could find, little shirts and gowns for Doctor Jim's baby, Miss Rachael sat at the big desk, the Old Doctor's desk, and wrote long letters. They didn't know where he was, but Miss Rachael wrote the letters anyhow (she said they gave her strength), and above her the stump of a candle guttered against the polished slats of the desk.

And then the baby. It was too early, only seven months, but Miss Rachael was standing in the door to her bedroom, her eyes black with fear as she clutched her belly and said, "Is it? Is it?" Jancy put Miss Rachael to bed, that big dark bed with posts that loomed way up to the ceiling, and she'd counted the pains and held the chloroform to her nose and when the baby started out, she held his head up over the bloody sheets until he was born. A tiny boy it was. With hair just as curly and dark as Doctor Jim's. And a little face so sweet and pretty she couldn't believe it was dead. She held him up by his ankles to drain his throat. She stroked his little chest, no bigger than her hand, and she breathed into his mouth. Nothing. He never moved. She wrapped him in the cleanest thing she could find and laid him on his side with his head facing away from his mother. And then she turned her attentions to Miss Rachael. She'd never seen so much blood. The smell and the color and the feel of it was almost more than she could bear.

When she stood up, Miss Rachael was coming to and soon asked in a weak, faltering little voice, "Where's my baby, Jan. I want to see my baby."

"In a minute, Miss Rachael. I ain't cut his cord yet. You lay still now and don't give me no trouble."

Jancy unwrapped the little body and tied a clean strip of cloth around the umbilicus. And then taking a pair of scissors, after plunging them into the flame of a candle, she cut.

Jancy put him in her arms for her to look at and she always

thought he was just sound asleep. Then Jancy took him away for Miss Rachael to get some rest and when she came back later in the morning, Miss Rachael had gone, too. And then it was nobody but Jancy, poor little old Jancy. She'd done everything just like the Young Doctor had taught her to do. And still they had died. Both of them. She prepared to go with the news to neighbors, to bring them for the burying. But first she went into the parlor and took out the heavy gilt-tinged Bible from the Old Doctor's desk. She didn't know what to put in the Bible. She could read and she could write good as anybody. But when it came to picking names for a dead white folks' baby . . .

At last she put in her short printed letters under the flowing script above which read so poignantly:

*James Andrew Westbrook, Junior*
*and*
*Mary Rachael Delamouth*
*were united in*
HOLY MATRIMONY

Jancy, the little yellow nigger, put:

> *April 7, 1862*
> *James Andrew Westbrook, III, was born and died*
> *And Mary Rachael Delamouth Westbrook followed him*
> *into heaven shortly thereafter.*
> *In the name of the Father and of the Son*
> *and of the Holy Ghost. Amen.*

It was a long and hard task and her fingers ached, but she sat and finished it out to the last letter. Then she slipped the Bible back into the old roll-top desk, pulled down the slats, and locked it up tight. They were all dead and gone and the Young Doctor . . . didn't nobody know where he was. And there wasn't anybody to give her freedom. They expected too much, it was too hard. The years of bitterness welled up and flooded her dreams.

"Ain't nobody. Looks like you could of bring me . . ." Jancy shook herself awake. Beatrice was bending over her anxiously. She was so fat her head looked like it was just stuck down in the rolls of her bosom and her eyes seemed ready to pop out.

"Oh, God knows," muttered Jancy and straightened up. "You bring me somethin?"

"Yes, Mama. Here a can of peaches like you like. And here the paper I brung from Kulps'." Bea put the things in Jancy's lap.

"You know I can't read! My eyes is so wore out. Where that no 'count at?" Jancy peered into the yard, the can of peaches rolled to the middle of her apron and then dropped in a swag of faded plaid down between her legs. She clutched the paper to her chin and waited for Sunday Jo.

"You! Sunday! Get up here and read to Mama Jan." Beatrice went inside, letting the screen slam shut behind her. She came back out in a few seconds with a wad of cotton in her hand. "Mama, if I done told you once I told you a hundred times that if you'd keep this cotton stuck up here on this screen them flies won't be so bad." She stuck the cotton in the middle of the screen door and then returned inside to scale and dress Troy's fish.

When Beatrice came back out again, a platter of pale filets in the crook of her arm, Jancy was gone to sleep, dreaming against the slats of her rocker, oblivious to the stumbled and broken reading of the little Negro girl at her knee, her golden hands folded as if in prayer over the slick can of peaches.

# Eight

B UT IF WITCHES could rest and dream away and fade like evening into deepest night, their children lived in inexorable alarm, eternally watchful. Their eldest daughter, listening reluctantly, twisted a strand of copper hair around her finger and frowned at her companion, a companion who chattered and hopped about like a sparrow and sowed her seed with abandon.

Sunday Jo certainly was no alarmist by intent. Quick and sassy, stubborner than ten thousand mules, she kept matters underhand. Like that summer when her baby brother, the plump and cranky Lionell, had been with them in the Quarters.

It was hot and heavy and the afternoon lay like a smoldering blanket over the rows of cottages that clung to the mountain over Piedmont Aluminum. The smelter buzzed and hummed and occasionally an irritable sound, like that of pounding, rushing waters followed by exploding gusts of steam, resounded. That sound meant many things to Christa Kulp. For it accompanied the pouring off of the molten aluminum or it was the sound of hell and Satan's red furnace. Whatever it really was, she had grown so accustomed to it that should it have suddenly someday ceased to explode and bellow, she would have started up, like a sleeper awakened.

On this particular afternoon, Christa, Sunday Jo, and Lionell found nothing better to do than to amuse themselves by climbing through the window of Bea's front room onto the porch. All around the porch, Bea had plants growing in buckets and glass jars. At the base of the railing, she had an unusually large mass of ice plant, green and thick as a carpet. It appeared to seethe and steam in the heat.

The window the children had selected was long and narrow and stretched almost all the way to the floor, with no screens and no weights or pulleys to hoist it up. Bea kept it propped with a stick of kindling. Christa climbed through and was followed by Sunday. And then small Lionell had taken his turn. Clumsy and insensitive in his bulky overalls, when halfway across the sill, Lionell knocked down the stick of kindling. And in one whistling stroke of sunlight and dusty panes, the window fell upon Lionell's big toe and struck it neatly through the bone.

Lionell howled and rolled to the porch in a bumbling orb of denim. He sat up against the porch railings, dismembering the ice plant, and lifted his foot and examined it with great shrieks and wild utterances.

"My toe!" he squawled. "Look what you all done make me do!"

And while Christa Kulp stood gaping and chewing her nails, Sunday Jo, with all the dignity of a bronze Minerva, stalked across the porch and gingerly picked up Lionell's toe from the window sill. She brushed it off carefully, and, after extracting a few bits of green ice plant from her brother's bleeding foot, slapped the toe back on in its place. She said to him solemnly, "Now, shetcha mouth, Lionell Turner. We going to the doctor over town and get him to sew your toe back on to your foot."

And before Lionell could bellow again, she had plopped him

**in** his wagon and was jerking him through the Quarters saying **over** her shoulder, "Now, hold that toe!"

That was Sunday Jo. But the more Christa listened to her silly palaver, the more obsessed she became. It was one thing to stand on Bea's splintery porch, smelling the crushed ice plant (which seemed to smell exactly like Lionell's dark blood), hearing the boom and crash of spilling metal, and witnessing Sunday's immense calm. It was another to walk with her through Nantahala in late evening.

Obsessions, once planted in willing soil, grow abundantly until they overflow and run down, destroying both the soil and the seeds.

"Look. Somebody lost a doll."

It was old and ugly with a soggy cotton torso, so washed and withered by the rain that it looked like a sorry modeling in glum clay. The wig was gone. And the eyeballs were bleached out white.

Christa picked it up and as she turned it over, the eyeballs opened and shut, clickety-clackety.

"Ugly old doll," she said and threw it far into the trees. Then she shivered. And as she did so, she felt Sunday Jo's eye upon her. She drew back her hand suddenly to strike and was immediately appalled. She'd never done such a thing before in her life.

"You make me sick." The hand fell limp. They left silently through the darkening trees. Christa did not begin to feel better until Sunday turned off to the Quarters and she went alone through the summer twilight, down through Johnsboro. She met her little sisters. They all ambled along in the pleasant air. The street lamps began to come on one by one up and down the streets of Johnsboro. Every corner was laved in yellow light. The poles smelled of creosote and little splinters stuck out all around them. Bea had told Candie and Connie that if

they'd but water the light poles they would come to life and
sprout leaves. All one summer they'd patiently sprinkled the
pole at the corner of Lee and when nothing came of it, finally
gave up.

Christa smiled to herself. Everything was getting warm and
comfortably plain again. Then they turned into Lee Street and
went past the Byrd apartment. It was on the end across from
the Kulps'. Shrouded in cudzu, dark, the very sight of it
brought back Christa's old dread. Mrs. Byrd kept a high wire
fence around her front and back yards. The twins had picked
up a stick and were dragging it along the wire, making a
twang, twang noise.

"Get them damn brats away from my fence."

Christa looked up sharply and there was old lady Byrd with
her head stuck out of an upstairs window. Her hair was grey-
ish and twisted up in tight ringlets all over. Her face was very
pink and in the yellow lamplight from the corner, she seemed a
spectral figure. She wore loose plates and was always shifting
them around on her gums and thus appeared to be incessantly
chewing. She held the stub of a cigarette in her right hand and
the smoke circled upward, blending with her ringlets and un-
certain features.

Christa herded the little girls across the street and into their
own apartment. At the door she paused and looked back. Mrs.
Byrd was gone; the window blank and dark. "That old witch,"
she thought. *Witch!*

The door that closed behind her opened somewhere else,
opened inside her and led into an endless labyrinth of fear. At
night, the fiery crackles that leapt from her brush ignited the
simple bedroom with terror. And Mrs. Byrd, who slept and
snored in dreamless chaos across the gravelly street, never
knew her powers. Never saw herself sit in the corner of
Christa Kulp's bedroom and smirk with glowing red eyes. She
did not know what it felt like to walk the doll roofs of Johns-

boro, inflaming the inky air and sliding into the brains of sick children. Christa was afraid. She fretted and grew nervous. She bit her nails. She stuttered. She quarreled with the twins. Rose noticed and commented to Bea. But Bea just replied, "She getting ready to go through the change, I guess."

It was terrible to fear a white witch, one who lived so close on Lee Street and cussed out of the window and smoked cigarettes and kept out all the rest of the world with a palisade of cudzu. If it had been Jancy, a witch of color, golden and ancient, wrinkled, if it had been Beatrice she feared, it would have been easier. One expected witchery there. But this other thing was Lilith. A child gets used to Eve, good old mothery Eve with her modesty and her sorrow, her sweat of travail. But Lilith was like the spit of the snake in the night. She had been there before Eve, maybe even before Adam, and God Himself walked in fear of her.

# Nine

LINDA EARL did not walk in fear of anything. At least she didn't think so. Witches never entered her territory. But the blackouts did.

First there sounded the sirens and everyone in Johnsboro rushed about extinguishing lights. Street lamps went out, kitchen bulbs clicked, and the fashionable hour-glass lamps dimmed to darkness. The whole town disappeared from the face of the earth. Then for a long time, for a long, long time it seemed to Linda Earl Glenn, everything was as soft and rich as a piece of velvet. She and Darryl sat together on the studio couch in front of the fireplace while Michael fumbled about for a candle on the mantel. Then there was a tiny spurt of flame and their faces were briefly illumined like those of carolers on Christmas cards.

Linda Earl was ambivalent about the blackouts. For one thing, they gave her a good excuse for not doing any work like ironing or finishing up the dishes. But for another, the impenetrable silence nourished many a bothersome thought and made her worry and think and puzzle over things that were a lot of trouble.

Like that awful person Arnold Snuggs. He was a painter and

had been with the crew that came to paint the apartment early last fall when the days were still smoldering from August. At first she hadn't paid any attention to him. Carolyn had just been born about a month or so before and took up most of Linda Earl's time. But then that Arnold kept hanging around, hanging around, standing in the porchway, grinning at her, his paintbrush and bucket in one hand, his eyes sparkling and the thin black mustache glistening with tiny droplets of sweat over his curling lip.

"You're somethin, Mizz Glenn," he'd drawled. "Just somethin."

As she looked up at him, Linda Earl suddenly became aware that all she was wearing was a pair of very short shorts and a pullover. The way Arnold looked at her, laughing and talking like that made her feel she was all legs and bosom. It was terrible. She closed her eyes and leaned back on the couch. But that wasn't the worst part. She opened her eyes and focused toward the candle flame flickering on the mantel. Darryl's head drooped onto her lap and he began snoring funny little-boy snores, his mouth opened in a rosy triangle.

That morning she had been mixing a cake to take to the choir members' supper meeting, Arnold Snuggs was painting outside the kitchen windows. She had the radio on, listening to her favorite jitterbug station. A couple of times she played at dancing with Darryl, mostly just swinging the little fellow around. A treat that he enjoyed greatly and responded to by squealing at the top of his lungs.

"I swear, Mizz Glenn"—it was that awful Arnold looking in at them through the windows. "I swear, if I had a woman like you, I wouldn't never leave home." He grinned real sly and smoothed down each corner of his mustache with the nail of his right forefinger. Linda Earl noticed that his fingernails were shockingly long and pointed like a woman's.

It had flustered her so bad she beat all the air out of her cake and then had to sit down and mix up another one right there and get it baked and frosted before five thirty.

Michael had stayed with the children as he always did when she went to choir. But this was something special and it was late when they broke up at the church and started home. She walked away carrying the uneaten portion of her cake in a paper sack. At the corner of Main Street (the only street in Johnsboro not named for a general or a president), a convertible coupé pulled out from the curb and coasted along in front of her.

"Good evenin, Mizz Linda Glenn. Don't you want to teach me how to jitterbug?"

Her heart absolutely froze within her. Absolutely *froze* as she stared at the row of short white peglike teeth under a black mustache. He was alone, steering the car with his left hand while his right arm lay draped along the car seat, along the place where he wanted her to be! Oh, he was so vulgar, so easy. And the smell of his shaving lotion had been nauseating.

Even after almost a year, Linda Earl could still feel sick at the remembrance of Arnold Snuggs. She was relieved by the blackout and the shielding darkness. She almost wished Carolyn would wake up and start fussing so she could go upstairs and hide for a while. How had she ever got back home that night! She had run and run, dropping the cake in its paper sack and trampling over it, the hateful sound of Arnold Snuggs' laughter pelting against her back. Dear God. If Michael only knew. He would kill that Arnold Snuggs. Poor little Michael. He was so tough and fearless, standing up against everybody, arguing. And he was also so nearsighted that he had been turned down by the Army. Anyhow, though, they told him that his job with Piedmont Aluminum was considered vital to the war effort. But it still liked to have killed him. She glanced over fondly at Michael sprawled in his easy chair, trying to read a magazine by the feeble glow of the candle. She almost felt like going over to pat his hand.

Linda Earl relaxed and began to cast about in her mind for something more pleasant than Arnold Snuggs to think about. Like the war, for instance. That was why they had these blackouts. Because Piedmont Aluminum was very important making metal. Johnsboro could even get bombed. What was a bomb anyhow? Something like a firecracker, except a million times bigger and louder. In the newsreels at the show there were bombs dropping out of airplanes, sinking through the air, then disappearing in a cloud of smoke as buildings toppled over like flimsy stacks of cards. And later on, in the aftermath, as the news commentator always said, there were these people walking around in the mess, turning over bricks and peering through broken window holes or just standing before the camera looking blank-eyed in torn stockings and dark kerchiefs. They were viewing the wreckage, the man said.

For the most part Linda Earl did not really pay much attention to the war. It was a lot of trouble, like having to use ration stamps for sugar and gasoline. And having to use that awful-tasting butterine instead of real butter. It came in a cellophane bag, completely dead-white, with a little orange button in the center. You had to mash the little orange button and work the whole bag around like kneading dough to get it a butter-looking color. But it always tasted dead-white. Come to think of it, Darryl had never even tasted real cow's butter.

She looked down at Darryl asleep on her lap. The side of his head turned next to her knee was moist and his short brown hair curled into ringlets. His lashes were long, so very long. "Why, he's almost pretty!" she thought with a tightening in her throat and she tenderly pushed the hair back from his temple. Somehow she'd never had time to think Darryl was pretty before. She stroked Darryl's cheek and then, yawning, fell asleep herself in the warm lambent little room. The town of Johnsboro lay still as a mouse in the dark of the mountains, while overhead the midsummer stars flashed impertinently. Somewhere bombs burst and men hid in the ground waiting. Whole armies advanced and retreated. Thunderstorms gathered and shed upon the earth. Dew and rain and hail rose up from the sea and then fell back. The hours passed. The sirens blew again and the little town revived itself.

# Ten

AFTER APPRENTICE seaman training, he had been transferred to a cruising ship. The ship carried him from Norfolk through the locks of the Panama Canal to San Diego on the West Coast. Then from San Diego to Oahu and the *West Virginia*, a battle-ship embellished with guns and turrets and grey armor, built with speeds in excess of twenty-four knots, designed to deal out crushing blows and sustain equal attack. He was secure. He became gunner's mate, second class. Then first. Elizabeth wrote to him, her stiff little alphabet etching away over the delicate paper in pale blue hieroglyphics. And he answered, on the backs of postal cards reveling in palms and shimmering surf. Johnsboro spun away on the other cheek of the world, locked in its bees-comb streets, blacking out at the sound of the sirens, unmolested. The attack upon Pearl Harbor, several bustling years past, had been to him, lying stretched on the rug, a shrill voice emanating from warm radios that stood next the sofas, the news spitting in between puffs of cigar smoke and Sunday dinner belches.

Gene Boyette found it different and he liked it. All around him, on the beach, little Hawaiian kids stood in the tide pools eating sea urchin, dripping purple mess down their chins.

There were bare rocks and sharp cactus mingled in with the palm and lush mango. He worked in sweat and grit, feeling the creosote burning away his skin. He learned to eat raw fish. He saw the juice of a pineapple, freshly chopped and split on a wooden table, bleaching out white every board and splinter it touched. He sat in the cane fields with the gun emplacements. He strung barbed wire over the gritty, shell-sharp beaches, marveling, wondering, often cursing his pitiable ignorance.

There was a friend, a guy called Q. Quincy Smith from Ohio. Good old Q, a grabber from the day he came bawling into the world, clutching at the empty air with feeble red fists. Q and Boyette, they went to the Pearl Bar, dimly glowing in pink neon, island guitars oozing, unseen, out of all the corners. For a dollar, you could have your picture taken with a native babe done up in reeking grass skirts, both of you standing in front of a phony grass hut with piles of phony brown coconuts at your feet. A picture to send back home. The beer was never cold enough and smelled disconcertingly too much like urine.

"How come you in this racket anyhow?" Q nudged him, slopping the beer. It slipped down the fluted rim of the stein in a pallid yellow tide. Gene's answer, like everything else about him, his whole existence, was sufficient, orderly, to the point.

"Because I damn well wanted to."

Because he wanted to. A boy who grew up two hundred miles from the sea in a land of rocks and red gully, briers and dog fennel, a town of glimmering aluminum ingots, bauxite, carbon, and cryolite, a house of beaverboard partitions, hedged around in boxwoods trimmed off at the knee: this, then, was a sailor? He hated his answer.

"Okay, okay!" Q flicked the ash off his cigarette and looked around to check the babes. "Let's go." The steins clinked down on the counter and the neon blinked, stammered, then brightened pinker than before.

\*

She could have been no more than eleven, thirteen at the most. Filipino. With dark, ripe-plum, black eyes. Her body was sparsely smooth and brown with almost no breasts. She lay looking at him with pity. He had failed. He had failed miserably. "Two minutes," she reminded, her childish voice struggling with sympathy, "two minutes, the old lady come to knock." He sat on the bed, stupidly picking at the pattern in the worn chenille. He got up. He gave her the five dollars anyhow and she smiled. A little baby whore Filipino with hair stiff and straight and black as a coal pit hanging down her back, brushing the bony little vertebrae.

He didn't wait for Q. He walked to the beach. Far out the surf broke in a white boom on the reef and the royal palms shivered in the wind. He looked down at himself: he was white, all white, the trousers, the jumper, the cap: all crisply white and tied round with the smooth black neckerchief. He felt each hard cold bead of the dog chain sticking to the hair of his chest. He tried to think it all back to the scenes of his imprisonment, his torment and struggle. Dampness seeped through his white trousers. He took out a cigarette. The spit of the match was like the last sound on earth and the sulphurous odor mingled with the clammy saline taste of the Pacific sea.

He had sat like this before, eons ago, on the far side of the whirling planet, surrounded by sun-steeped clover in Virginia, watching his grandfather's windmill turn in the wind. And then the hawk had come, noiselessly, out of the impenetrable blue sky, intent, aimed. He soared high, his beak printed against the bare wide spaces, perfectly defined. The wings dropped and stiffened. The boy on the ground below sat still and listened to the sound of the hawk and the creak of the windmill, turning, scraggelty-scraggelty, turning and pumping with power. Silvery water leaked out of the seams of the wooden tank and moss coated the tower legs. The hawk came on, stronger now, and as the boy watched, thrilled, the bird seemed destined for the hub of the turning blades. Then, in a bursting-bubble-clear moment, the wings raised and propelled the body upwards and over the windmill. The force of the air through the feathers made a threatening unearthly hiss.

Far out, the ships rode at anchor. The surf crashed and tumbled and the palms behind him bent. The cigarette went out in his hand. When he returned to the ship, he found his orders were to be sent state-side to a gunnery school in Washington. Before he left, he had his picture taken with the Hawaiian girl at the Pearl Bar and with Q and some other guys. These he sent, generously, to Elizabeth. Elizabeth turned over the new photographs. There was Gene Boyette, immaculate in Navy whites, standing before a grass hut, a pile of coconuts at his foot, his arm thrown wantonly around the naked shoulder of a native. Another showed her three sailors squatting on the luxuriant lawn of the Royal Hawaiian Hotel, the wind slightly ruffling their satiny black neckerchiefs. It had been almost two years and she'd had time to think. Elizabeth Boyette picked up the dictionary off the table beside her chair and stuck the pictures in the deepest part of it. Homecoming would be interesting.

He was lucky and made the right bus connections between Washington and Charlotte. But from Charlotte to Fairview, he had to thumb, standing by the hot asphalt road, each car that passed showering his clean trousers with a moil of dust and field chaff. Once in Fairview, though, he was again lucky to run into a man from Johnsboro, Jim Kulp.

Riding to Johnsboro with them, Gene was conscious of the stale hamburger-and-onion smell that clung to his clothes. The three Kulp children, all girls with red hair and almond-shaped grey eyes, stared at him. The older Kulps talked of the usual things. Jim asked all the regular questions about the Navy and the war and the islands, and Gene gave him all the regular answers, and they all laughed at all the regular jokes. Then there was a lull. Gene sat looking out at the Palmer County farms gliding past his window, listening to the hum of the automobile and the droll chatter of the little girls behind him. Green, brown, honey-bright, a herd of cattle standing in the shallows of a dark three-strand creek, and then sunlight bright and rapid as any bolt of lightning: it passed before him in lovely profusion. He thought of the time when, as a little fellow of maybe five or six, he had been riding in a car with his dad. He had held a glass jar on his lap and inside it buzzed a honeybee. Gene had looked upon the bee buzzing in a circle of glass and then thought of himself riding in a vehicle of steel upon a ball of earth that was revolving within limitless air. He had gotten quite ill and vomited all over himself and his dad.

"Boy!" Edward Boyette had exclaimed, "why didn't you *tell* me you were sick!"

Gene shifted his weight and then asked quietly, without pretense, "Do you all ever hear anything of the Byrd girl?" He turned and looked at Rose Kulp, wedged in between him and Jim, her left knee scraping against the gearshift.

They seemed to speak at once.

"Oh, she went into training, you know, right after the war started. Liked to have killed the old lady. She's so darned queer, you know, and stingy. She made quite a fuss. But we don't see her too much any more. I heard Mrs. Thomas speaking only last week . . ."

"She's in Fayetteville. At the Army hospital," Christa broke in from the back. She leaned her chin on the edge of the front seat and gazed at Gene.

"Well, that's what we've all heard," said Rose. "Of course, you don't ever get the truth much any more. But I did hear

Mrs. Thomas tell something about Rebecca being home for a while." She turned to Jim. "Did you hear that?"

He nodded and then they continued silently down the road to Johnsboro. Christa gazed intently at the sailor in front of her. She observed how his color changed ever so slightly at the talk of Rebecca Byrd. The tips of his ears were bright red in the sunlight. His cap sat at a jaunty angle. And his hair was very blond. His eyes, well, she really couldn't see his eyes too good, but they were surely dark. Maybe dark blue or brown. But quite dark, too dark for such golden hair. His face was tanned and an identification bracelet glinted in the hair around his wrist. She liked him. She even liked the smell of him.

At the corner of Stuart and Lee, Gene got out. He offered Jim Kulp some money for the ride, but Jim shook his head and said, "It's the least I can do for a man in the service." Gene smiled and waved goodbye. The last sight he had of them was that of a solemn-eyed little girl with long coppery hair peering at him through the dusty and finger-marked oval rear window.

When he phoned in to Johnsboro earlier, Alice had said, "She layin down right now, Mister Gene, but I get her if you say." And then she had waited politely for his direction. Gene knew in his mind how she looked, too: standing by the Queen Anne secretary, holding the phone to her right ear and cradling her elbow in the palm of her left hand, her head drooping just a bit to hear better.

"No. Don't. But when she's up, tell her I'll be in as soon as I can. Look for me when you see me."

"Okay, Mister Gene," said Alice and hung up the phone. And then there was nothing but empty silence. Now, as he opened the screen door of the apartment porch, there was again nothing but empty silence. A thin grey fold of ore dust lay across the porch, even capped the railings. Gene pulled the door shut carefully and set down his canvas bag. Then a furious barking erupted from the living room and Gene Boyette was held at bay by a tiny bandy-legged dog.

"Hush! Pablo be quiet!" Elizabeth came forward. "Well, hello, honey." She embraced him and patted his shoulder. "How are you?" She steered Gene through the door and into the living room. The little dog, still growling, retreated to the cushions of an armchair, his big round eyes glowering.

Gene stood blinking in the middle of the room. It all seemed the same. There was the Queen Anne secretary with the telephone; the dark piano near the stairway (he had always pulled down the shades whenever he practiced); brass tongs and shovel beside the fireplace, and over the mantel a crayon portrait of himself as a plump child dressed in (how ridiculously apt) a little white sailor suit. It was as he had left it. But Elizabeth. Her new enthusiasm alarmed him. It was so out of character. Elizabeth was never, never aggressive. It made him stiff, suspicious. But then Alice came in from the kitchen, smiling shyly and nodding. And Gene felt at home again. He gave Alice a grass skirt and a pillow that had long red fringes and embroidered letters reading "Hawaii, Island Paradise." She shook out the skirt and held it to her waist, laughing and exclaiming, "Why, Mister Gene! You should not a done this!" And she was obviously pleased that he had.

"I thought you'd make a good hula girl, Alice," he teased.

"Oh, not me!" She took her presents and, after thanking him again, went back to the kitchen, bowing as she departed.

To Elizabeth he gave a tiny box carved from monkey pod, the famed wood of the islands, smooth and richly toned, durable as oak. There was a fish design upon the lid, a fish with long flowing fins and rings of delicately etched scales.

"Why, Gene," she said, opening the little box. Inside was a pair of earrings. She took them out and held them on the palm of her hand. The soft luminous hues of rose-gold and blue-pearl wavered like lanterns under water. She looked up and found she had no voice in which to thank him. The very sounds of it would seem imperfect, out of place. It was no boy, fresh out of high school, no naughty child in a closet, that stood before her. He was a man. And the ties that she had cautiously begun to loosen during his absence fell open, the stone was rolled away.

When Edward Boyette came home from work, he embraced his son and shook his hand with pride. Dinner was a calm, quiet affair, though Elizabeth seemed gayer and almost had a flush in her cheek. Alice served them without a word, as usual, and below the windows, the African violets bloomed and spread their wistful beauty, silent and serene and without purpose.

Every bathroom in Johnsboro had a tub of grotesque Chippendale design. Huge and formidable, these things sat on ball-and-claw feet, filled from a pair of rickety brass spigots, each one thoughtfully labeled (in thin black script on tiny porcelain plaques) as HOT or COLD. The Boyettes' was no exception. Everything was close and cramped. Any real convenience was but an afterthought. A person sitting in the tub could reach out and touch the lavatory with one hand and the commode with the other. A small window, cut directly in the middle of the back wall, afforded the only ventilation. A naked light bulb dangled down from the ceiling.

Gene settled back in the hot bath and studied his toes sticking out of the water at the other end of the tub. The soap floated and bobbed about his knee. It was very white soap and a very brown knee. His whole body, from head to loin and from thigh to toe, was brown from the suns of Hawaii. Those rich, high-flung suns, never too hot, always welcomed, even when your back was aching from swabbing deck or mending lines. Gene sighed and leaned his head on the rim of the tub. It really hadn't been too bad, this homecoming deal. Elizabeth had been okay. Not at all the way he'd expected. And so far no damned asthmatic attacks and no red pills. He felt the water gurgling around his ears and he closed his eyes.

*You must think*, he told himself. Think of blue water rising in swells, deep, blue-dead water, eddying in white, the pearly bubbles bursting in your nose with a small barely perceptible click. Water, bare and naked, virginal and cruel water. You lean your cheek inward to be stroked and the blue-glass swell mounts and devours the black etching of the superstructure and the radar antennae.

The ship is underway. The word is passing: Man Overboard. They are breaking and half-masting the five-flag, their fingers on the halliards, with several shrill blasts on the pipe, they are passing the word to the officer of the deck.

Rapidly drifting now. The swells rise and crest like wing-stretched birds, like hawks or gulls, then gently drop, wings folded, spent out, beaten. The copper-covered buoys in the racks amidships have been dropped. You think with a wry smile that it was probably Q that pulled the toggle. Ahead of you the calcium flare pots are showing light as soon as they hit the water. Ah, Jesus. Sweet, salty, little blue-tailed Jesus. Think. Now.

You are no place in the world. The water, cold and unyielding, is still blue, blue as milk-of-magnesia bottles you found up under the house. The sun glares. And the smoke pots trail thin red whispers, as thin and as red as the rust on an old tin can. Those cans, pierced and crushed through the belly, they fall in a silver mass to the breast of the blue bobbing sea. When the ship is underway, the manual plainly reads, in times of unrest, refuse is not to be thrown overboard to leave a trail. Garbage, litter, and slops are to be carried to the honey box. Metal cans are to be pierced and crushed under the ten-pound T-shaped bar in the dull grey iron sink and cast over the side to plunge to the bottom of the sea.

Think of yourself. Cast over the side. The calcium smoke eddies upward and the sun glints on the mangled cans. I cannot make it to the big buoys. I do not want to make it.

Q will tell them in the Pearl Bar, smirking over a chipped stein, "That crazy goddamned little Boyette. Tied that T-bar with his belt. Who'd of thought he had that much gut in him. And the whole time that damn Carter is standing by with his finger up his butt, not paying no attention."

And they would all laugh at what Q had said about Carter.

Dovetail after dovetail surged and foamed, ruffling in the wind and bursting against the steel, churned from the bottom of the ship.

It was no good to think. He shook off the sleep and opened his eyes. He was back here again in Johnsboro with Elizabeth.

As the water chortled and whirled down the drain, he got out and rubbed himself vigorously with a towel. It was lavender. Elizabeth had always insisted on lavender towels. She even wanted the bathroom painted lavender, but the paint crew had never heard of lavender. So it was painted cream like every other bathroom in Johnsboro. But the hamper, wedged under the tiny window, was enameled lavender. And the window was hung with lavender and on the sill bloomed another of her precious African violets. Gene pinched off a purple blossom. The tiny stamens crumbled in his hand, as yellow as the yolk of a hard-boiled egg. He stuck the violet behind one ear and looked at himself in the mirror. Then his breath steamed over the glass, and, wrapping the lavender towel around his waist sarong-style, Gene Boyette went upstairs.

Upstairs in his old room, the corner one with a fireplace, he opened the bureau and looked at his civilian clothes lying there all neatly folded. He took out a short-sleeved shirt, then considered the sultriness of the night and put it back. He'd just go in his T shirt. In the closet, he found old moccasins; and clad in these and some well-worn, almost white, jeans, he padded downstairs and through the apartment. Edward was reading his papers in the living room. He glanced up briefly as Gene went through and then nodded absently. Elizabeth was lying down somewhere and the dog Pablo had vanished.

The screen creaked as Gene pushed it open with the toe of his moccasin. Outside the sweetness from jasmine bushes hung all over the yard and a chorus of cicadas was making merry with their stiff-legged, chitinous, hard-shell and dry-winged music. At the curb, he stopped to light a cigarette and then continued walking down the street.

Overhead the sky was starting to sprinkle with white pin-pointed stars and there was a slight breeze burdened with jasmine and after-supper odors. Children were still playing on the sidewalk and on the apartment porches people sat in swings or rockers, fanning themselves with folded-up newspapers, flapping at the mosquitoes, and quarreling with the children.

Gene turned off Stuart Street and started down Lee. Mr. Kulp was out watering his grass. The sprinkles fell across the pavement and it seemed to sizzle from the heat it had stored up during the day. Gene stopped and chatted for a few moments with Mr. Kulp. He noticed that the two littlest girls were twins and asked them their names. "Kate!" "And Dupli-Kate!" they shouted in turns, then broke into giggles. "No," they sobered. "Mine's Candie." "And mine's Connie." "And we're catching lightning bugs. Looky!" They held up a Mason jar with several sparkles of yellow inside. Gene peered closer and saw there were indeed a number of lightning bugs crawling about. "Phew." The little twins wrinkled up their faces. "They stink terrible!" Then they scrambled off and Gene said goodbye to Mr. Kulp. As he moved away, he saw the other one, the older one, lying on her stomach in a porch swing, her chin on her hands, watching him. He gave her a wave of his hand and she broke into a wide toothy grin.

A little farther along, he met a young woman with curly brown hair and a pretty face. She pushed a baby in a stroller. The baby was dozing, its little head bobbing against the tray of the stroller, and a little boy followed behind on a red tricycle. "Come on now, Darryl." The woman shook her hair back from her face and frowned. They all disappeared behind a broad hedge of obelia.

At the very end of Lee Street, on the corner across from the schoolyard, stood the Byrd apartment. Gene walked on around it, casually flicked his cigarette on the cement and stepped on the lit end. There was no sound and no movement from the apartment and the yard was empty. But as he turned the corner, he saw at a glance a lamp glowing under a beaded shade and a white-headed old woman sitting in the lamp glow and near her, standing tall and lovely, Rebecca.

He crossed over the street, no longer Lee, but now South Main, and walked into the schoolyard. A rack of swings dangled empty in the darkness. At the drinking fountain, he stopped, stepped on the pedal, and bent his head over the arch of water. After wiping his mouth on the back of his hand, Gene strolled to the swings, chose one, and sat down. His moccasins made a soft pat-pat in the dust of the yard and the chains creaked and smelled of rust. In a moment he was still, watching the apartment across the way. "God," he muttered, reaching for another cigarette, "I must be some kind of a nut." The tobacco seemed mute, insensitive to his taste and he threw it down. "I really must be a nut. Sitting out here in this crumby swing looking at that crumby apartment and waiting for a girl I've never said one damned word to in about a hundred years. God!" But still he sat.

Presently Rebecca came to the door and said (he could hear every word as clear as a bell and yet she spoke quite low), "Mama, I'm going downtown a minute."

"You going leave me again!" The old lady squawked like a parrot.

"I'm just going to the drugstore and maybe the post office, Mama. I'll be back soon." And she opened and shut the screen matter-of-factly upon the old woman's noises. "Bye, Mama," she added over her shoulder and set off briskly down the street toward town. Gene Boyette watched her until she was out of his sight around the big red Theater building, and then he got up, too, and followed in her wake.

# Eleven

HELLO, REMEMBER ME?" He stood at her elbow; and his voice sounded ridiculous in his ears.

"Why—" She turned and looked at him a moment, remembering, then gave a little chuckle and said, "Why, yes. You're Gene Boyette. But you're supposed to be in the Navy."

"I'm still in the Navy. But right now I'm in gunnery school up in Washington and I got a few days' leave." He paused and glanced around. "Sit down?"

They were being reflected from four angles in the plated mirrors behind the counter: far left, left, right, and far right. Rebecca's hair was pulled high in a swirl on the back of her head. Her skin seemed whiter than ever and her eyes glowed with all the lustrous smoothness of black marble.

"Sure."

The reflections flickered away. They sat down in a booth.

"Care for a cigarette?"

"No thanks." She watched as Gene struck a match. He lit the cigarettte, then looked at her over the still-burning flame.

"And what about you? Aren't you supposed to be off having all kinds of wild adventures in the nurse corps? Sawing off arms and legs and all that sort of stuff?" He settled back against the booth. It was upholstered in a leather the color of mahogany, bound at every edge with hard little tacks. The table between them was topped by glass and a little wall lamp glowed cosily under a yellow shade bordered by pheasants and hounds and men on horseback. Rebecca laughed.

"Oh, sure." She followed the flick of ash from the cigarette. "And I suppose it will be worse than that when Mama and everybody else in Johnsboro gets through. But I don't care."

Doc Tracey shuffled out from his dispensary and began turning off the big overhead fans.

"I guess he's fixing to close."

Gene snuffed out the cigarette and stood up for her to pass. The mirrors reflected two pairs of twins, one blond and one brunette, going out the door. Doc Tracey pulled down the long narrow shades behind them. And the electric clock on the wall, the clock that advertised Dixie ice cream, said the hour was half past nine.

In the darkness, sweating upon sheets and pillows bordered with delicate lavender, Gene Boyette dreamed. He was on the roof. A boy. In the middle of a midsummer morning. One of those hot mornings when laundry flaps on the line smelling of suds and strong bleach. And a host of brown children run barefoot through the grass, sidestepping honeybees. And dogs bark furiously. And behind it all the hum of Piedmont Aluminum wallows in the lowest decibels of a warped tuning fork.

A bead of sweat trailed down his nose and into the flare of a nostril. The bricks at the bottom of the chimney, the place where it cut into the roof, were sheathed in moss. And as Gene grasped at them, his fingers broke away leaving long green smears. All around him were spread the shingles, the rose-colored shingles, shaped like great flat diamonds, as precisely fitted one upon the other as scales upon a fish. Before him the roof rose sharply to its summit and below him it sloped away in a long angle to a point where he could no longer see the tips of the ladder resting against the wall.

He couldn't go up and he couldn't go down. He was suspended, helpless. "Alice," he croaked, fearing to shout and maybe lose his balance. "Alice?" But Alice was whistling over her ironing deep within the house beneath him. With one masterful burst of effort and gut, he turned on his back and was immediately jolted by fear, staring blankly into the sky above, clutching at the rose shingles with desperation in every fingernail. He lay there indefinitely, mute, and immobile, listening to the sounds of the world. He lay there so long that he fancied he could hear the very ants crawling in the grass and each crumb they carried grated upon his ear with all the dissonance of an earthquake.

"I can't get over," he told himself. "It's too hard."

A grocery truck rattled up the back alley, stopping then starting again in a rhythm alien to the boy on the roof. The sun beat down on his face until he closed his eyes seeing little bubbles of effervescence float about in his eyelids. They drifted and darted and devoured one another like translucent protozoa seen in a drop under magnification. The smell of bruised moss crept upon him and blended into the smell of the sun and the rose shingles draining out every cell of his flesh.

"I'll just fall and let myself wake up. It's only a dream. A dream."

And then the noon whistles blew stridently out of the hum of Piedmont Aluminum, a harsh banshee wail that shook the marrow out of his bones, and he sat up, awakened, peering into the dark bedroom, bewildered and relieved.

He got out of bed. Beyond his window, the moon had sunk way down west and all was quietness, darkness. Outside, the town of Johnsboro lay still, breathing in its sleep unafraid. The screen felt cool against his face and he pressed it hard and thought of the girl pressed against him hours earlier. She was cool, too, without being cold. And she was quietness, darkness, breathing unafraid. In a strange moment she had led him through the bypaths of his rapture into an incredible region where nothing was in its place and reason became obsession. Gene shuddered. And then he smiled. Alice would have said, "A possum jumped over your grave, Mr. Gene." It seemed heresy to even think of it now.

Rebecca had once been made of ivory, a figure to be adored from afar, from the dim back pews of the cathedral where only now and then the incense drifted and the faithful knelt until their bones ached and their pointed hands grew stiff. Her face had flickered from the glow of vigil candles set at her feet, but now he knew her to be made of a different stuff. Not ivory. And not wax. He had reached out for her in wildest daring and she had taken him. And in those moments he had felt his soul being seized out of him. Her hair, her Filipino hair, spread across his shoulder, had tickled and smelled of violets and honeysuckle and the tiny yellow roses that curl wantonly over back fences in spring. But then she had left him suspended, in a state of punishment, left outside of himself. And now Gene Boyette wondered. He wondered and for the first time in his life began to grow afraid and unsure. His boyhood plights, interrupted and rescued by the workaday whistles, had suddenly returned in all their dizzying charm: the hiss of the wind in the hawk wings, the attraction of the blue swelling sea.

Gene stood before the window, alone and dark as a canyon. In the east a faint streak of light seeped through. This lovely seizure must surely end. And the balance be restored. The vertigo cured.

# Twelve

Seizures and sudden confiscation, accompanied by both blinding dizziness and sharp comprehension, came to everyone in the time of the great second war. And in Johnsboro, the town made of dollhouses and honeycombs, Gene Boyette of Stuart Street and Oahu was not the only one to suffer. In another part of town, another balance was being wound, coiled, and set. The seizure here, however, was not rapture, but discontent.

One of the things that gripped Michael Glenn so much about his being turned down by the Army was the fact that he came from a family of Pilgrim Guardians and most all of them were conscientious objectors. This rankled him day and night. He felt the people of Johnsboro, the whole world, the outermost galaxies, placed him in this ignoble class. And the agony of it was that Michael Glenn had striven all his life to dissociate himself from the rest of the Glenns and from the whole kit and caboodle of Pilgrim Guardians.

As a child he was taught never to salute the flag, never to pledge allegiance. "Idolatry of country," said his mother, a thin-lipped shadow of a woman who never put paint to her face or cut her hair or consulted a doctor in times of fever and pain.

"You've only got one birthday," she quietly explained, tearing up an invitation to a party, "and that's the day you're born."

His brothers, his uncles, his cousins, his now-dead father, all gave two years of their manhood to the preaching and propagating of the Word. They stood on street corners and knocked on doors and collected dimes for a pinch of salvation. Michael grew up hating himself and his heritage. He knew there were greener pastures, so he made the break. He joined Mission Church and made himself comfortably Presbyterian. He went to work for Piedmont Aluminum. He married Linda Earl Little, beautiful daughter of a prosperous Palmer County farmer. A girl who did put paint on her face and who consulted a doctor at the vaguest sign of discomfort and who looked as pink and white as the pinkest and whitest of birthday cakes. And he tried to join the Army.

"May God in all His righteous anger strike you down," said his mother. "How glad I am that Dad ain't here to see it. See his own flesh and blood turning away from the true living Christ and going out to the ways of wickedness. I knew you'd turn out bad from the first time I found them tobacco shreds in your pocket. Go away. Don't never show me your face no more."

And he didn't. He made good money at Piedmont Aluminum. He had a good-looking wife and soon two children. He didn't need *them*. At evening, sometimes, he and Linda Earl drove about Palmer County. And over in Fairview, on the edge of town, stood the Temple, a low ugly building covered by imitation-brick paper. Once they passed by and saw the congregation inside rising to their feet all at once. A fat bald man stood at their head, gesticulating, and the skin of his skull had glistened under an electric bulb hanging at the end of a black cord.

"They're probably in there handling snakes and speaking in foreign tongues and all the rest of it," sneered Michael. He gunned the motor and rocketed past in a gust of litter and gravel.

"Do you know how my daddy died?" And before Linda Earl could shake her head, he had interrupted and was jabbering hotly. "He had an in-growing toenail and it got infected. And then it got worse and started to rot his foot and then went up his whole leg. One day I went in there to put a cover on him and his leg was white. The next time I saw it, it was black. And the whole time he lay in the bed and rotted, Mama was there reading her Bible and praying and then reading the Bible some more. And then he died and she took all the money we had and sold furniture, sold our bed, *our* bed, now mind you, and buried him with it. Every time I slept on that cold hard floor, I thought about my old man and I hoped to God he was sleeping good." He looked at his wife, all pink and white against the seat of the car. She just sat and stared at him, her brown eyes round and dumb. Things that rotted and turned black and smelled bad never occurred to Linda Earl.

"And do you know something else?" Michael was talking more than he had ever talked in his life. More than he had ever opened up to this lovely soft creature beside him. "My stupid mama told me that she didn't think God intended for us to go to the moon! Or to Mars! Or even to California, which to her is about as remote as the damned moon." He laughed and accelerated the automobile. "I hope to God if anybody ever goes to the moon, it's me." He laughed again.

But he really could not shake them. He had to do a big something, bigger than going to the moon. His car gave him power, his money gave him power, his lovely wife and children gave him power. But not enough to shake the Pilgrim Guardians and the Glenns and all the humiliation and fury born up out of a lifetime. It really had to be a big something.

At the beginning of the war when he volunteered, he had been turned down on account of his bad eyesight. But now the year was 1944 and he tried again and was accepted. He came home in the afternoon jubilantly.

"I just quit work, Linda, just plumb up and quit. Just like that. I walked in there to Mr. Nashley and I said, 'I'm quittin, Mr. Nashley.' And he said, 'Well, aren't you going to give me any notice?' And I said, 'I'm giving you exactly fifteen minutes!' "

Linda Earl was perturbed. "Oh, Michael! How could you?"

But he was firm. And when he kissed Linda Earl goodbye at the bus station in Fairview, his face wore a look she'd never before seen. It was the look of inner communion, that direct light from Heaven that shimmers full force upon a man who has passed beyond human senses and intelligences. "Oh, Michael," she said again, tears welling up in the corners of her eyes. But then he was gone. She stood alone on the black tar-and-gravel street looking blankly at the disappearing bus, tears running down her cheeks in little glittering veins. Then, taking a dainty handkerchief out of her purse, she went back inside the bus station. Crying was becoming to Linda Earl. It made her brown eyes more luminous and her pink cheeks pinker. She stopped before a mirror hanging beside the ticket counter and took good notice of these facts, dabbing at her eyes with the handkerchief and fluffing out her hair before passing on.

But back home in the apartment on Lee Street, she felt the greatest loneliness of her life come upon her. She grew remorseful and wished she'd been nicer to Michael back before all this came about. She sat down on the studio couch and blindly watched evening lengthen into shadow. Next door she could hear Beatrice getting ready to go home. The Kulps had generously offered to keep Darryl and Carolyn for her while she went with Michael to the station in Fairview. And tomorrow she must think about moving back to Mother's. But right now Linda Earl could only sit there, alone in the darkening and empty apartment No. 42, putting off meeting faces again.

She looked around the living room. It was not right. It was not hers any more. There was the piano, tall and dark, hauled from her father's on the back of a pickup truck.

"Why do you want this thing? You won't ever get time to play it. And the children will scratch it up something terrible."

"I don't care! I just want it. It's mine. I want it!" It was too heavy, too big, too richly black. But she and Michael and her father had managed to shove it back into the alcove beneath the stairs where it forever after sat in lonely splendor, its three brass pedals gleaming and the ivory gathering dust. Linda Earl suddenly got up, crossed the room, and sat at the piano. She struck a key. It was cold, dusty, and the sound wavered into nothing. A key, a felt-tipped hammer, and a tensed wire. Music. Michael did not like music.

And where was he now? Riding through miles of North Carolina country. Through Piedmont and sand hill, forest and farm, passing under the glow of neon, past littered road banks, and city dumps, cemeteries on the hillsides, old houses, new houses. On to Fort Bragg. And beyond Bragg, the War.

The street lamps began to come on and the yellow glow fell through the windows onto Linda Earl at the piano. She looked down at her hands upon the keyboard. They were soft, delicately wrought at the wrist, and the ring on her left finger shone demurely against her skin. She stared at it and began to feel very spiritual and quietly enduring, but still uncommonly afraid.

The mind moves to its own music, displacing, fulfilling, incessantly questing. Linda Earl's mind moved to an evening in late autumn. She was a child and Granny Little was remembering when she herself was a child and about the Yankees and wintertime. And there had been a moonbow. Anyway, that's what Granny had called it. A huge white circle stretching out from the moon making the sky bright with ice crystals for a hundred miles in all directions.

"We set in the middle of the floor all wrapped up in a quilt while Ma tipped around from winder to winder a-lookin. A-lookin for Yankees to come and burn up the house and us in it. It was so cold. Ma wouldn't make no fire and we like to have purely froze."

They were sitting in the side parlor, just off from the kitchen, sitting before the fireplace. Mother was mending: one hand deftly slipping the darning egg into a sock and the other casting, casting, overcasting. She broke every last thread between her teeth. And Linda Earl, no older than six or seven, was stretched on the floor, buttoned in a white nightgown, the side of her that lay before the fire was warm and rosy and the side away from it was cold. Granny got up and stood in front, knotting her hands behind her back.

"Ever time I remember that night, I get so cold I can't hardly live. After a while us children got to tusslin under the quilt. Florence scratched me. She always had the longest fingernails of anybody in the family. And she had me hemmed up under that quilt and was a clawin at me like sixty. So I let out kicking and accidentally kicked Benjamin along with Florence. Then he jumped into it and brung Willie in with him. And poor little Pearl started crying. She was the baby and Ma's favorite. So Ma come over there then and jerked the quilt off'en us and commenced to whaling butts. She said, 'If you younguns can't sit together like folks, then just stay apart and freeze. I hope everyone of you gets froze to death by morning.'"

Granny laughed and turned around. "Wan't no use arguing

with Ma, so we all slunk off and pilfered around for all the cover we could find to wrap up in. I had the quilt off'en me and Florence's bed. It was one Ma'd made before she's married. Somethin called toad-in-a-hole. I always liked it bettern any cover we had."

Granny had sat back down and was rambling on in her tale, not caring who listened or didn't listen. Linda Earl turned her other side toward the fire. When she laid her hot cheek to the floor boards, they felt startlingly cool. Mother kept on mending and breaking off threads with her teeth.

"I tipped over to a winder in the front room. It was so bright outside with the moon shining on that snow. Our house stood down in a little holler-like place and the woods rose on either side. I ain't never seen the like of that snow piled up around the house and under them trees. And the trees were casting deep blue shadows all across the snow and down through the holler. I kept on lookin and thinking 'What if a Yankee was to come? Just pop up out of them woods?' I imagined a whole swarm of 'em appearing on the ridge in front of me, all frost-covered and lit up by the moon. I thought I could even be able to see the breath from the hosses' mouths and smell it and taste it, too. Before long Ma tipped up behind me, Pearl fast asleep on her neck, and said in a low voice, 'Liza Mumpford' (she always called me by my full name), 'Liza Mumpford, you seen anything?' 'No,' I said. And she went away to look out from another winder.

"I looked and looked until my breath clouded up the panes and melted and ran down in drops. I kept wantin to see somethin. It would've been bettern just standing there watchin for nothin. I'd of rather been burnt up and kilt than just gone on standin there freezing to death in the dark." She broke off shortly and sighed.

Linda Earl rolled over and sat up at Granny's feet. Granny

was wearing old felt slippers, the color of burgundy, and her skirts came to her ankles. "What happened? Did they ever come?"

The old woman roused herself and blinked dumbly at the rosy child before her. Then she collected herself and smiled and said, "No. Didn't nothin ever happen, honey. Next day the snow started to melt and before long our pa come home, all wore out and muddy. We soon had to start the planting. I hadn't seen my pa in such a long time that I asked Ma one day who was that man." She chuckled. "But that's the way it was. We got used to it, I reckon."

Linda Earl Glenn sat in the shadows, her music faded. "I can't get used to anything," she thought bitterly. And then she began to weep uncontrollably; and this time it was not becoming.

# *Thirteen*

Summer passed into autumn. The waters of Lake John returned and Piedmont Aluminum continued to murmur incessantly, producing rows and rows of gleaming ingots. Darkness brought the blackout drills. John Murdoch's people slept and waked and grew older, grew seasoned by war and routine, finding refuge in their shingled honeycombs. Those apartments of Johnsboro had perhaps achieved the ultimate. No one lived above or below anyone else. It had to be either to the right or to the left. A man's roof top was his own. They stretched like one tremendous long and narrow house coming to an end at the corner of the street and then continuing on the other side to zigzag, circle, and turn endlessly throughout the town. And the tenants of the house, though divided among hundreds of paper-thin compartments, could have, had the notion ever struck them, tapped gently upon the wall before them and the echo of that tap would have resounded through every wall in Johnsboro and shaken the very perimeters of the world.

But there were changes. Michael Glenn was gone; and so were his wife and children. "I'll be staying at Mother's now," Linda Earl had told Rose Kulp as she prepared to leave. "But I'll be over town sometimes and I'll come by." Rose patted her hand and hugged the children. Beatrice baked Linda Earl a cake to take with her. "Thank you, Bea. I'll miss you." "That awright," Bea said. "Troy's gone to the fightin, too. I be missing everybody."

The seasons passed, unaffected and indifferent. Winter came. In the middle of Johnsboro, at the convergence of the generals and the presidents, stood an ancient cedar. Tall and durable, older than Lebanon, older than John Murdoch and Mission, it suffered its foliage each December to be decked and studded with strings of colored bulbs. Johnsboro was proud of that tree. Not for being cedar, not for being strong and old and unyielding, but for being each year a Christmas tree. In the first moment of brilliance, as the waters of the dark Yadkin churned through the dams of Piedmont Aluminum and excited the wires and flamed the tiny bulbs red and blue and green, the people stood enraptured. Then they went away and the vision of that gigantic pyramid illumined in rainbow burned in their minds all year.

At night the small streets echoed with carols. The days were pale and grey with crackling frost and a sun that weltered like a medallion reflected upon a sea of mirrors.

Christa Kulp had decided to put away the nonsense of Sunday Jo and last summer. But one night, the night before Christmas Eve, she dreamed she was being drowned, her bed swept away on a swift red river. It flowed gently at first, eddying with soft sucking, rocking her timidly. Then pieces of the bed had begun to fall away and the bedclothes crumbled like clay. Christa was left with only a shred, a splinter of a bedpost to sustain herself against the red currents that rushed into the room, divided and then came together in tremendous swells. All night long she was tossed, pulled down into the channels and propelled like a cork from a bottle. In the morning she woke as from a sleep of poppies. There was nothing but frost splitting against the pane and tepid sunlight. And under her bed, only dust.

She rose and looked from the window. The cudzu clung to Mrs. Byrd's apartment and looked like dried dead blackened blood vessels. The circulation seemed stopped and, like a limb deprived of its blood flow, the house had gone into a troubled sleep.

December passed. Linda Earl did not come to Johnsboro very often. Christa Kulp went to school and passed before the blankness of her old enemy day in and day out. Gene Boyette was back in Hawaii.

The water never lost its fascination for him. He stared at it endlessly, from the deck, the turret, on the beach. He went into it, his eyes goggled behind a handmade mask of glass lenses rimmed in wood, banded around his head by a rubber thong. The slip of the blue water went over his body with the touch of a thousand hands. Overhead the sun weltered. He came up, treading water, shaking the bright drops from his yellow hair. Down again, deeply, into the still chambers of iridescent fish and vaguely moving seaweed. Q had found a conch here, a big one, veiny and gnarled in dark orange. He brought it up and set it on an anthill. In two weeks, the ants had picked it clean through and through. Gene looked for another one.

Ahead, bellying with the rhythm of the waves, he saw a huge grey shape. He halted, feeling fear prickle through his flesh, warning. It was not familiar, but threatening, and persistently silent. It came toward him methodically, unhurried, opening and closing itself like a big monster morning-glory, then it snagged on the sharp butt of the reef. In the same instant that he had felt fear rising along the back of his neck, Gene had recognized what the grey shape was. It was a target sleeve, a long muslin hoop, thirty feet of it, shot down by the practice guns, floating and sinking, harmless. He grinned to himself under the water and darted upwards. He came ashore and removed his mask. In the tide pools, warmed by the sun, still teeming with fish and tiny crustaceans, he found a cowrie, leopard-spotted, smooth and comforting. It succumbed to his hand. And he took it for her. The water knocked gently at his feet.

She took the cowrie out of its cardboard packet. It was smooth as an egg and oval and creamy-colored with dark brown spots. And as she rubbed her fingers over the whorls it pleased her greatly. Not quite so wide as the palm of her hand, it still seemed rather large to have come in so small a box. She closed her hand over it and it was warm without being sticky. Rebecca put the cowrie beside her and began to write.

Dear Gene,

Thank you very much for the cowrie. According to the dictionary the cowrie is a marine gastropod and is used in some countries as money. Also as a good luck charm. I hope it brings me luck. I love it. It is so pretty.

She stopped. It was silly, useless and silly. She crumpled the paper in her fist and threw it into the basket under the desk. He had sent the shell without a word of any sort. Just the smooth leopard shell. She would accept it with the same silence. That would please him, she knew.

The window was open at her elbow and she leaned forward. Right across the street was a big old-fashioned house trimmed at the eaves in gingerbread-lace. It looked ridiculous, so innocently sitting there in the middle of town, surrounded by a big busy impersonal hospital and black asphalt parking lots. The shutters had faded from green to a hazy aqua wash. And with its two giant cedars on either side of the walk and its iron fence and crumbling birdbath, it seemed a part of another long-forgotten, put-away-in-mothballs world. Rebecca sat

there looking at the remarkable old house, all the more remarkable because she realized she had never really noticed it before
this evening, and suddenly there appeared in an upstairs window a little girl with blond hair, straight and fine as cornsilks.
She stood and looked out between the bristling cedars and she
sang "When Jesus was a little boy-ooooy." She stood and sang
and her hair shone like pale gold. Her voice was exquisite for
one so small. She sang the song through twice, then, shaking
her straight cornsilk hair, she was gone and the window
loomed silent.

Rebecca withdrew her elbow, still blinking at the old house.
She felt sad, heavy as lead, her chest caved in, too full. In its
packet, the cowrie glistened. He was strange, his crazy senseless faintly horrendous dreams of water and roof tops and
hawks and barrenness. He was strange. And last summer she
had liked what he told her of the little Filipino. She had not
been angry with him. It pleased her to remember. The Filipino
whore-child and Gene. She tried to place him there on the
island, in the blue water. But she couldn't. All she could see
was Johnsboro, rows and rows of grey, flat apartments, the
slopes rising full of them, chimneys smoking. And his stiff,
prissy mother. Her loud, vulgar one. The trials and terrors of
saints. She thought more and grew more despondent as the
darkness began to descend. Things he had told her nodded
about in the room, vagrant philosophies he had speared up out
of the tropical sea.

Whatever it is the world has dreamed itself into being, it is
our job to find out. No, that didn't sound right. As children, he
explained, twisting a strand of her hair, we are taught to pray
each night for safe passage through the darkness. And yet we
know, as surely as we know the intonations of our own voices,
that the morning will come; and if not a morning, at least a
something. No, again no. She brushed them away.

In Johnsboro, she had never prayed, never been taught the

smug safe words to dispel the black night. The world had merely gone on turning and in the morning her feet would be cold where the blanket had slipped.

Rebecca got up and prepared to dress for duty. Yesterday they had operated on an old woman who had mothered fifteen children. Doctor Kearns had asked her, good-naturedly, as she was going under the gas, "Which one of your children you love the best?" Her answer floated up, lame and timid in the room of steel, "The one that's sick till it's well and the one that's away from home till it's back." And she had expired on the table before the hour was out.

Outside it had grown quite dark. Street lights flashed on and automobiles glowed, bumper to bumper, in the parking lots. Rebecca pulled down the window and without hesitation slipped the cowrie into the pocket of her cape. She went out, still sad, unhealed and unable to expire.

Christa Kulp could not have known about cowries and obsessions. But she was soon to know charm and danger as never Rebecca Byrd or Gene Boyette would.

It was spring and at school they were giving a May Day. The first grade would be honeybees, the second grade would be elves, and so on. Christa's grade, the sixth, were to be some kind of Grecian dancers or nymphs. And Beatrice had to make Christa's costume. It was of thin green gauze with a girdle of paper roses. There was another thing of gauze and paper to go on her head like a little wreath. Bea grumbled and spluttered over her clumsy needle.

"Ain't never heard tell of no such going-ons. Traipsing around in this here rag. Must be some of that no 'count Vanhoy's doings."

Bea had never cared much for the principal of the school, Mr. Vanhoy, since he had fired her brother-in-law from the post of janitor last winter because he was sleeping on the job and letting the furnace go out and getting the pipes frozen and causing a general disturbance all the time.

"Yessir, some of that no 'count Vanhoy's doings for sure." Bea threw the flimsy garment across the ironing board and went to pour herself a snort of Jim Kulp's bourbon. She could do this in front of Christa without any qualms about exposure. The twins would have tattled the moment he came in the door. But Christa couldn't have cared less.

Beatrice washed it down with Coca-Cola, carefully rinsed the glass, and started to press Christa's costume. After a while, as her veins warmed to the bourbon, Bea sang and sang and scorched the gauze.

> *"From all the dark places,*
> *Of earth's heathen races,*
> *Oh, see how the swift darkness flies!"*

She went back to the cupboard to refresh herself, went through the rinsing procedure again, then picked up the iron and continued.

> *"Rescue the perishing!*
> *Care for the dying!"*

(Each note sounded like a hen house in the midst of a tempest with all the hens giving birth en masse.)

> *"Snatch them in pity from sin and the grave;"*

With her eyes rolled heavenward and both massive hands rooted on the iron, Beatrice gave her all:

> *"Weep o'er the erring one, Lift up the fallen,*
> *Tell them of Jesus the mighty to save!"*

At the time for the Second Refrain, Christa rose from the chair where she had been reading and said, "Oh, Bea! Can't you touch a drop without getting plumb drunk? And you're scorching my costume, too. Mother always says she can tell every time you get in the likker 'cause she'll smell scorched clothes as soon as she gets out of the car."

Beatrice put down the iron, jerked the plug from the wall, flung the gauze tunic onto a wire hanger, then drew herself up like a monstrous brown toad and spat.

"I ain't drunk, Miss Priss. And if you's to know anything at all about drinking, which you don't, you'd know the difference between being drunk and being high. I is high. And I is glad of it. I need somethin to restore my soul after pilfering with this here costume all day. Now, I going cook supper and leave it warming. Then I going home where I can be amongst sensible folks. You watch the stuff after I gets it fixed and keep them twins off'en it until Miz Rose get here. Is that clear!"

Christa nodded and said, "Yes, Bea." She was sorry that she'd put Bea in such a bad mood. There was no use in trying to make up, so she slipped out of the kitchen and wandered out of doors. She flopped down in the porch swing. Candace Leila and Constance Lucille were off somewhere at a friend's house. They wouldn't be back till supper. The swing creaked. Across the yard a breeze sprang up and ruffled the green cudzu of Mrs. Byrd's apartment on the other side of Lee Street. She hadn't seen Mrs. Byrd much lately. Not even all last winter, it seemed. Last summer, Gene Boyette and Rebecca had walked right down this very street one night and kissed over there on the doorstep. She'd seen it from her window. She wondered what old lady Byrd would have to say about that. The kiss of the prince that broke the spell of the enchanted sleeper. The stroke that felled the witch and put away the darkness. That's the way it was in the fairy tales, always.

The longer Christa sat there, swinging softly and staring over at the rippling green cudzu, the stronger her thoughts became. They grew on her like a coral reef, each cell slowly solidifying into a stony mass of sharp obduracy; and the waves of a shining sea broke upon her endlessly. So obsessed was she that she did not even notice Beatrice hustle to the door and say goodbye.

It was not yet dark, or even shadow, but somewhere up on Murdoch's Mountain a whippoorwill set up hollering. His hollow cry rolled over the stony child below and reinforced her. Old lady Byrd probably *was* a witch after all. She was bound to be. Anybody that old and ugly and hateful couldn't be anything else. There was nothing nice about her. Except Rebecca, maybe. Christa softened a moment, thinking of Rebecca. But then she hardened again. How could such a terrible old person like Mrs. Byrd have such a beautiful daughter like Rebecca?

Maybe she was dead. A sudden shiver of elation shot through the child's soul, and she got up from the swing. If Mrs. Byrd was dead, then her spells would be dead, too. And so would Sunday Jo's. It was all her fault anyhow. Damned little nigger. And Rebecca would be forever free. And she herself, Christa Rosemary Kulp, coming-up-twelve-next-birthday, could walk through the darkness unafraid. It all seemed so exquisitely easy.

Once she was out of the yard and across the street, Christa had lost all fear. It fell away from her like an outgrown garment, as flimsy and meaningless as the green gauze inside the kitchen. Old lady Byrd, witch, demon, mistress of hell, was now no more to her than a curious old trinket to be examined, something as insane and harmless as a virulent spider caught and strangled in a lump of amber.

The door was closed, but at her touch it fell open as easily as though she had the force of iron. Christa stepped into a room of odd assortment. It was dark, curtained by omber velvets, most of which were faded and thready at the edges. On a long table before the windows stood a number of photographs in ornate frames, ovals and oblongs, scrolls and cherubs. And as she peered through the dim light, Christa was startled to see, once her eyes had adjusted themselves, how distinctly someone's fingerprints were stamped upon the brass. All the little threads of the thumb, the canaliculi of the fingertips, coiled precisely, one beside the other, and seemed to smirk at her from their reddish shadows.

Beyond this table of photographs stood a wide Japanese screen papered in vague blues and crimsons, showing mountains ascending to cloudy oblivion and limpid pools set round with trees in bloom. Down one corner of the screen trailed a thin piece of torn paper, as thin and vague as the landscape it had failed. Christa stood drinking in the strange gloom, marveling to herself that this was but one chamber among countless others in the maze of Johnsboro, yet it was so frighteningly different. It was the castaway, the great Unseen talked about and paid tribute to but never witnessed; it was the fearful and naked edge of the world.

She moved forward entranced and then her breath froze within her. All the while she had been standing there dumbly taking it in, looking and pondering, she had been half-conscious of a wheezing rhythmical disturbance to the left of her, in the deepest shadows of the room. It was much the same way one gets used to hearing the hum of a household machine or the engine of an automobile and only partially responds. But now, as she focused her eyes on the figure behind her, she realized with a plummeting heart that the disturbance she heard was the sound of Mrs. Byrd, snoring, asleep on a brown velvet settee.

It was cold, oh so very cold. Outside, the early heat of the season glowed in the rays of a melting sun. But here in this sad chamber of velvet and Japanese paper, finger-stained brass, dust, gloom, and climbing cudzu, it was as cold as a polar midnight. Who could stand before such cold? Who has indeed entered the courts of the Snow Witch to claim the return of innocence? Who among you can warm me? Speak!

The longer she stood, the colder she became. All her fears so newly shed in the golden evening—the safe golden evening that lingered beyond the door—came swiftly back. After an indefinite period, an eternity, an ice age, Christa found herself slowly coming to life again. Blood bubbled through her veins, warming the snow-flesh, thawing out her courage, and she moved. One short step backward through the door and she would be free. She felt for the doorsill under her foot and began to slide back.

"What?"

It was the old woman herself, waking, struggling from sleep, sitting up on the little settee.

"Who is that?"

She reached over the back of the settee and pulled the chain of an enormous lamp. Its light flooded over Mrs. Byrd's frowzy head and gave a sheen to the brown velvet. She sat up straight and smiled tenderly at Christa.

"Why that's Becky," she said. "Little old Becky Byrd. Come here, honey. Mother's been waiting on you."

The old lady reached out her arms to Christa, stunned in the doorway.

"Come on," she wheedled, begged, a smile trembling at the corners of her mouth. Christa could only stand and stare. Stare at the smile on Mrs. Byrd's mouth and at the places where she had smeared her lipstick. It was very orange and crumbly lipstick. With supreme effort, the child averted her eyes and fixed them on the lamp behind the old woman. It was old and massive and the bell of the shade drooped like some grotesque and wilting blossom around its slender pole. The shade was beaded with tiny pieces of glass and these beads followed the pattern of a tortoise shell, large at the border and descending into diamond-shaped stars across the apex. Below the lamp, on a high table, round as any barrel in a farmyard, sat an ash tray in the shape of a green frog, his mouth perpetually opened to receive his mistress's refuse.

"What's the matter, Becky? Why don't you come on in, baby?"

"No, mam, you don't understand," Christa began politely, then faltered. Her voice belonged to the frog and to the mammoth lamp; her syllables choked on ashes and stumbled along a yellow path of broken tortoise.

"I'm not Becky. I'm Christa Kulp from across the street." She swallowed and, with another masterful stroke, took her eyes from the frog and onto Mrs. Byrd. The smile wavered and hung to the edges of the old mouth.

"Becky!" The eyes were hard. "Come here!"

"I'm not Becky! Please!" The child turned and fled, a torrent of curses sweeping behind her through the glimmering curtain of cudzu and into the street.

"Damn your soul, Becky Byrd! You never been nothing but a harassment to me since the day you're born!"

She ran and as she ran great gulps of fear and disappointment rose up within her. The apartment, empty, still smelled of Beatrice's supper warming in the oven. The green gauze fluttered against the pantry door. Upstairs Christa ran and, locking the door behind her, fell full length upon her bed. But the tears did not come. She lay in wait. But she was unrequited. Evening advanced upon Johnsboro and the whippoorwill on Murdoch's Mountain was joined by other birds in his plaintive search for loveliness.

Across the street, behind a weave of whispering cudzu and omber velvet, Mrs. Byrd still sat on her little settee.

"Why, it's getting dark," she remarked to herself, blinking. Then she rose to shut the door so rudely left open by her young visitor—a visitor she had forgotten. In the glow of the lamp, her hair appeared to be a web, a froth of white and grey. She put a cigarette to her orange mouth, struck the match, and began to pick up the photographs, one by one, and then put them back down, one by one.

# Fourteen

IT WAS OVER. Michael Glenn, sailing across the Irish Sea, had
been struck by a German torpedo and blown into paradise. It
would have pleased him more to have died battling his foe
hand to hand, bloodstained and reeking with the smell. But
dead he was anyhow. And in full uniform. His widow was
present at the unveiling of the war monument, June 1947, in
downtown Johnsboro. Everyone was there.

Linda Earl was bewildered. She'd hardly had time to get
used to Michael's being in the Army when he was suddenly
killed and all she had left of him was a piece of yellow paper
from the War Department. His body could not be recovered.
It lay at the bottom of the sea. And now, almost three years
afterwards, she found herself standing on a hot afternoon in a
crowd of folks looking anxiously up and down Main Street for
the Honor Guard to approach.

The monument stood in a little park, newly mown and
neatly bordered by hedge. Linda Earl noticed the grass had
stained her white pumps and she felt a dull ache start between
her shoulders.

"Yonder they come," said someone next to her. And soon

the Honor Guard marched stiffly into view and stood at attention while some preacher uttered a small prayer for the souls
of the sacred dead. Then a little girl dressed in white organdy
stepped up and snipped a ribbon tied around the canvas that
shrouded the monument. Men pulled away the canvas and the
Honor Guard raised their rifles and fired. After the shots had
died away, the hum of Piedmont Aluminum droned on monot-
onously.

The monument was not pretty. A grey lump of stone,
chiseled at oblique angles, it strove ambitiously to give the
effect of a great unfinished work of sculpture. Linda Earl
squinted as the sun caught upon the gleam of every bronzed
name. People were sobbing quietly and looking grim, so she
took out her own handkerchief and dabbed at her eyes. But
there was no remorse left in her. Michael was in the sea and on
a piece of stone. The letters of his name would be rained upon,
dusted by the passing of vehicles, washed by snow, and
warmed by sunlight. His body would be eaten by fish and
perhaps someday those fish would be caught on a hook and
also eaten. Oh, it was so confusing. Linda Earl turned away,
then turned right back. For one last look. "I must remember it
all for the children," she said. Her brown eyes watered in the
piercing June sun and the dull ache in her back turned to real
pain. Since she had no sorrow, she wished desperately for wis-
dom or for fortitude. She felt Granny Little would have understood her as she now at last understood all that had been
Granny.

"Won't you please come and take dinner with us?" It was
Rose Kulp, her long-ago neighbor of Lee Street, that long-ago
when all of life had been discontented and fruitless beauty.

"No, thank you, Mrs. Kulp." Linda Earl smiled into the
woman's kindness. "Mama's waiting on me with the children.
But thank you, anyhow." And she went away, her white shoes

splotched with green, her handkerchief a crumpled ball in her hand. It was not Johnsboro that she left, not Michael Glenn on a piece of rock, but a whole way of life, an unveiling.

Bea was washing. The whanging machine reverberated in every corner of the apartment and Bea's voice caroled stridently over it. The twins made tiny boats from toothpicks and tried to sail them in the tubs of bluing.

"Get out of there!" squawled Beatrice. "You mess up my bluing. And you liable to get a arm caught in the wringer! And then we have to call the doctor up here to saw off your arm!"

"Oh, Bea!" said the little girls. "Ain't no such thing going to happen!"

"Is too!" Beatrice scooped the frail toothpick boats off the bluing water. "Now go tell Christa and Sunday Jo to get in here. I'm ready for these clothes to be hung out." And she swatted at them with a cloth.

It was nice outside to be hanging up the clothes. The sun shone down on the tops of their heads, so hot that it almost blistered their hands to touch up there. The sky was blue as Beatrice's tubs. And when they had pegged all the wash and left it winging in the wind, Christa and Sunday Jo, with the help of the twins, took an old pink counterpane and draped it over the grapevines and sat at ease underneath.

"Who planted these here fox grapes?" asked Sunday Jo, jerking at a green cluster.

"Nobody," answered Christa. "Nobody that I ever knew of. They've just always been here." She lay back on the ground looking up at the sunlight filtering through the pink threads.

"I help Bea plant a grapevine over in the Quarters and we got grapes off'en it that big." Sunday made a huge O with her thumb and forefinger.

"Pshaw," said Christa and closed her eyes. She fell asleep.

And soon did the Negro child and the little twins. In the house, Beatrice dozed over her kitchen table. It was after lunch, in the middle of a brilliant day. Sunlight fell across the pink tent. The vines twitched as birds paused, then pushed away for better perches. Ants traveled the ridges and scars of the thick vine trunk. And dogs, running down the alley, halted, forepaw raised as in salute, wet nose testing the air for scent of the slumbering children. But on they slept, their eyes sealed. Doors opened and closed, automobiles passed along the street, other children laughed in other yards, and the sun shone splendidly upon eave and roof. Once Christa started in her sleep, her fingers trembled and she made a little moan. Sunday Jo smiled in hers. She saw angels and they waved to her, "Hey, Sunday Jo. You cutish thing." The twins slept with the trusting abandon of infants, white throats vulnerable, the silent pulsations under their skin continuing uninterrupted, fearing nothing. It was not the day for death or trespass.

The trees on Murdoch's Mountain were so thickly grown together that the first spatterings of the rain did not reach the ground for almost a full minute. For the greater part of the afternoon, Gene and Rebecca had climbed steadily, over vines and broken pine boughs, picking their way by tremendous granite boulders scattered along the mountainside in a giant recklessness. Now that they stood on the top, looking out over the auburn flow of the Yadkin, it was almost a feeling of let-down, a depression of spirits, that accompanied the raindrops falling on them.

"Gee," said Gene, wiping his face, "now I know what it means to say 'I've climbed a mountain.' "

Rebecca shielded her eyes from the rain which was growing harder and swifter. She gazed and gazed and then sighed deeply. The golden afternoon had turned grey, bluish, even weird. And what was even weirder was to be standing here, on top of Murdoch's Mountain, in a pelting rainstorm with Gene Boyette.

"Hey!" he shouted. "Let's get out of this stuff. Come on." He jerked her along behind him. They slipped through the woods and into a partial clearing, where the mountain really flattened out into a sort of table. Ahead were the ruins of the Murdoch place, a house, a shed, and an old cellar built into a mound of earth and brush.

"In here!" The house was all but gone. A few remnants still clung to the chimney, but the timbers of the roof had fallen. Of these there was formed a sort of crude triangle with the old chimney standing as its median. The wooden shingles, the fallen slabs, though rotting and weak with age, offered a refuge from the merciless rain.

They stood shaking the drops from their clothes and looking at the ruins about them. The old fireplace was blackened and sooty and the mantelpiece that had once stood above it drooped like a broken wing. The stale smell of the hearth was suffused in a fierce freshness of summer rain and as the bright drops fell down the chimney and struck the ashes, they made a puckering sound.

"Let's build a fire," suggested Gene.

"Why? It's not cold."

"I know. But it'd be so cosy." He began to scrape around for pieces of dry wood and debris. There was much of it stuck back in the crumpling corners and soon he had a pile on the hearth. He struck a match to it and smoke curled for a moment around the edges, then it blazed. Rebecca drew near and sat down. Her eyes reflected the flames and she sat as one transfigured, exalted by the fire and the sounds of the rain, enraptured.

"Hey." Gene knelt down, still rubbing at the rain in his hair. "What are you thinking about?"

She broke her stare and laughed absently. "Oh, nothing. I

was just wondering what poor old Preacher Murdoch used to think about. When he sat in front of this fireplace. Or"—she got up and passed to the broken doorway—"or what, when he sat out on the porch and looked at that mountain."

"Probably about religious junk. There's a bunch of papers and stuff of his down at the church. We looked at it once. On Rededication Day. I think maybe there is a diary he left, and things like that. Oh, I don't know, though." Gene poked at the little fire and sighed. "Sometimes I feel like him."

The girl turned back from the door. Beyond her the blue rain fell in sheets and dazzled the woods. "What do you mean?" she asked softly, coming to sit beside him again.

"Oh, being happy and not being happy. Knowing what I want and not being able to get it. Or maybe not even wanting it at all. It's crazy." He laughed, nervous, feeling exposed and drawn out, shy.

"How do you know he was like that?" Rebecca leaned her dark head upon his shoulder. The fire hissed and sputtered as raindrops fell into it down the chimney.

"Oh, I don't really. But it seems likely. I mean, why would he come off up here and live if he wasn't unhappy? Why didn't he live down in town? Or go back to Scotland?"

"I don't know much about preachers and churches. Mama is an Unbeliever, you know. I've only been inside Mission once, when I was little, and she wanted to show me what it was. We went in and it was full, couldn't see a place anywhere. The preacher was already up preaching. But Mama stomped on down the aisle and halfway down she stopped and hollered back at me in the vestibule, 'Come on, Becky, here's a place!'"

She did not know how to go on and fell silent. The silence grew, accented only by the pattering of the rain. She spoke again. "This doesn't seem like July ought to be."

"Nothing seems like it ought to be any more. When I accepted my discharge, I guess I thought everything would just go on like it had been in the Navy. It took me all the way from Oahu to Johnsboro to finally get used to it."

The hair, hanging blackly wet and flaccid down her back, yielded under his hand. He wound it around and brought it together about her throat.

Down into the dreams of darkest midnight, into those hours when only the old sit alone and stare into moonlight, down deeper than the drowned sailor, they plunged. It was all dark, with echoes and many whisperings, the fire sighed on the hearth beside them and the rain lashed in crystal frenzy against the grey shingles.

An arrow went out into the heaven and it was not fairer than my love. It fell and the shaft was broken. But my love flies swift. He forces the wind as a young hunter forces the bow. He does not falter. And when it is over, in the evening, and all is hushed, my love approaches with the bird in his arm and my heart swells.

When raindrops began to pellet the pink counterpane, Christa woke with a start. Beatrice came to the back screen and squawled, "Get in them clothes, quick!" The children roused immediately and began pulling the dry laundry from the line and running with it to the porch.

"Just leave the pins on the line!" said Bea as they dumped their burdens in a basket at her feet. "I do hate and despise for my clothes to get wet once they got dry."

"We ain't going get these clothes all in, Bea!" hollered Sunday Jo, banging the screen behind her. "It's fixing to pour!"

And indeed it was. And it did. Half the laundry was left on the line, dripping and deplorable. Beatrice eyed it through the screen. "I do hope Mama in," she said enigmatically.

But Jancy was not in. Nor was she on the porch, dreaming in her chair. She was in the yard, standing there holding on to the porch rails and smiling. "Why, Rachael!" she exclaimed.

"Yonder you do come. Little barefoot. Little barefoot." She smiled so broadly, her eyes beginning to brighten as old tapers suddenly being lit, that her face was an exquisite mask, the mask of Comedy. "Oh, Rachael. Is that my freedom you bringing, honey?"

Jancy moved forward without tottering. And the fierce thunderclaps she heard were exactly what she had expected all these years. "I'm meeting you. Jancy's here, too, you see!" Across the yard she went, that bare yard that Beatrice kept so carefully swept clean of stones and grass, and she opened the fence without even looking at it. The rain fell upon her, streaming down the golden skin, but Jancy laughed and licked at the bright drops.

At the end of President Lincoln Street was a drainage ditch swollen with the heavy rain. She never saw it or felt the water surging about her. She saw Rachael running to her. Little barefoot. And behind Rachael, the death angel. Oh, snow-white destroyer with wings of gold. Jancy smiled. His hair flowed in purest white and when he turned his eye upon her, it was of pearl.

> *He gives snow like wool;*
> *he scatters hoarfrost like ashes.*

Through this water, through this everlasting and lovely water, over and over the frail body was tossed. They recovered it almost half a mile from where she fell in, it having been forced by the swift muddy flow through two large culverts. When they pulled her out, the rainstorm was over and the late-evening sun shone royally. It caught the gleam of one thin earring that still dangled delicately from a lobe of golden flesh. She was ninety-nine years old.

> *He sends forth his word, and melts them;*
> *he makes his wind blow, and the waters flow.*

*

It was quite dark when they came down from Murdoch's Mountain. The rain had ceased before sunset when Gene put out the fire. It was almost chilly. A bird shook down more rain on them as they passed under his tree. It was slippery in the forest and they descended with care, skirting the Yadkin, crossing over its many creeks and gurgling streams, all filled to the banks by the storm. When they stood at the edge of Johnsboro, the lights had begun to appear and the town seemed a blanket of fireflies.

Down they went through the heart of town, past Doc Tracey's drugstore, past the baroque red Theater, and at the post office, across Main Street from the war monument, they paused. Steam rose from the pavement and the smell of new rain swelled the night air. At precisely seven fifteen o'clock, the red-and-yellow Pathways bus rolled to a stop before them. Rebecca got on, paid her fare, and sat down, dark head bending close by the window. She looked up once as the bus circled in front of the war monument and then drove steadily away, down Main Street, and out of Johnsboro. Gene watched for a while. The lights of Piedmont Aluminum burned broadly in the night and occasionally a burst of orange sparks could be seen within the rows of potrooms. Lake John cuddled placidly at the side of its mother, Yadkin. And the Yadkin flowed on endlessly without heed.

On Lee Street, in the upstairs window, sat Christa Kulp. Her room was dark and she sat looking out upon the night. Starlight shone on her pale cheeks. Below her, raindrops still dripped softly from the trees and the trees themselves were covered with millions of fireflies. Johnsboro twinkled and glistened, clean, fresh, unpretentious.

She would not learn of Jancy's death until tomorrow morning. She would not hear that Rebecca Byrd had gone away and Gene Boyette faded and both of them maybe forgotten Johnsboro by the time she might hear.

Raindrops sparkled on her screen, reflecting the street lamps. Tomorrow they would be melted, sucked up in the light to make more clouds and more rain. It was irresistible. On the mountain, high above Christa Kulp and the town and all the doll cells, slept John Murdoch, an alien to his earth. Upon his plain gravestone, a single raindrop traced the fading letters of his name.